"These are service dog patches, Daisy," he says, holding up tiny round pieces of colorful cloth. He doesn't squeak. His voice is dog-treat serious. I pay attention.

"You have your vest," he says, and points to my uniform. "If you pass your service dog test, Victor will sew these patches on your vest. Then you'll be a true elite. A real service dog. I want you to be an elite dog, Daisy. I want you to earn these patches. We have nine weeks, Daisy. Nine."

He tucks the delicious patches back into his pocket.

An elite.

The Colonel's grip on the leash tightened when he heard that word, so I understand.

An elite is Important. It's special, unique, different from just *pet*. It's a tasty word, like chicken. Elite is useful.

I was told I was useless by the other humans, my first pack, and then they left me in a Dumpster. I'll do everything I can, toenails to tail tip, to be the opposite of useless.

I want those patches so much I can feel it down to my paw pads.

Elite.

KRISTIN O'DONNELL TUBB

A DOG LIKE
DAISY

KATHERINE TEGEN BOOKS
An Imprint of HarperCollins Publishers

★ DEDICATION ★

*To the families who serve our country
(because when one family member serves,
the whole family serves)
and to my family,
who continually inspires me to be brave*

Katherine Tegen Books is an imprint of HarperCollins Publishers.

A Dog Like Daisy
Copyright © 2017 by Kristin O'Donnell Tubb
All rights reserved. Printed in the United States of America.
No part of this book may be used or reproduced in any manner what-
soever without written permission except in the case of brief quotations
embodied in critical articles and reviews. For information address
HarperCollins Children's Books, a division of HarperCollins Publishers,
195 Broadway, New York, NY 10007.
www.harpercollinschildrens.com

Library of Congress Control Number: 2016960212
ISBN 978-0-06-246325-8

Typography by Andrea Vandergrift
20 21 22 23 PC/BRR 10 9 8 7 6 5
❖
First paperback edition, 2019

★ 1 ★

HOPE LIKE FIREFLIES

The cage I'm in squeaks when I move, and the sound makes me picture tiny scratches of the color yellow, like toy lightning. Plus, when I shift, I lose the warm spot I've made on the metal. So I stay still. You can smell and hear things best when still. The colors tell you more.

Quit moving, the Doberman in the cage next to me snaps.

I didn't.

Well, then quit thinking about moving.

I snuff. These cages are no way to build a pack.

1

Humans know nothing about the importance of building strong pack dynamics.

The bell over the Good Side door chimes green.

Good morning! Howdy-do! Hi, hi, hi! The dogs and pups greet the incoming human.

"Morning, Daisy!" Janie says when she gets to me. She stoops to my cage and reaches in. My tail thumps, because petting is a joy like sunshine.

Janie's voice is creamy thin milk. Janie. That's the tag of the Woman in Charge around here. She scratches me behind my good ear. "She's a good girl."

I am. I am a good girl with one good ear. Useful and good, despite what my old pack said.

The Other Worker comes in next. His tag is Phillip. He squats on his hindquarters to my bottom-row cage. Refreshes my water. Then leaves. Phillip doesn't look me in the eyes or speak. Ever. I only know the tan color of his voice by his clipped answers to Janie. But I don't get the feeling he's evil.

Janie in Charge and the Other Phillip are nice enough. The shades that color their speech and shine on their faces are usually pale, like a cold-weather sunrise. Certainly not bold, so probably not useful.

The bell over the Good Side door rings again, and three humans enter, two full-grown people and a pup. A boy. The cage above me wiggles with glee. *People! People! Lookee here! Lookit me!* the puppies yap.

People make things interesting, because they can take us Out. A soft glow of hope lights inside me like a firefly. Yellow, but not too yellowy. Hope, but not too hopey.

The bell quiets. There are two doors in this room. One has a bell above it. The bell shows that it's the Good Side. From my cage, I can see through the clear Good Side door. The Good Side has sunshine behind it. It smells like grass and earth and rain and garbage and running and freedom.

The other door in this room is thick and metal. It slams when it closes. Echoing slams, like trucks with jaws. Dogs who walk through that door smell like fear. Those dogs never return. It's the Bad Side.

Rumor here is that each dog gets fourteen sunrises before they must go through the door to the Bad Side.

I have two more sunrises before I have to walk through to the Bad Side. I know that means I should muster my cuteness for these humans, but I just can't do it. False enthusiasm tastes like salt water.

The three humans who entered pause at each cage. Two of them, the full-grown adults, don't reach through to pet the dogs inside. Unusual. Most humans say chewy pink bubblegum words like *ooo* and *lookee* when they peer in at us. Most of them want to touch each one of us, which mixes our scents and makes us smell like dog poo stew. Most of the humans' voices change to the color of a sunny sky when they visit us, their words rays of sun.

But these humans are different.

Even the boy. He doesn't reach inside the cages; he doesn't coo. But his eyes smile. He has a soft glow of hope inside, too. He has fireflies in his heart, like me.

"So, what are we looking for, exactly?" he says.

The Biggest Adult turns. He's standing apart from the other two. He walks with a limp and a stick. "A dog. You know: Four legs? Fuzzy? Preferably no fleas?" he says, and tries a laugh. No one laughs with him. The statement falls short, like an underthrown tennis ball.

The Biggest Adult sighs. "They tell me it will help, Micah." He talks like snapping twigs.

The third person is awkward. The Awkward One is not part of their pack. I can tell by his smell; he smells like wild onions, while the other two smell of the same soap. The Awkward One clears his throat. "It will, Victor." Ugh. His voice is a pinched paw. "And

I think this dog looks like a good possibility." The Awkward One reaches in to Snuffles's cage. Snuffles is a bulldog mix. He grunts a loud *howdy-do*.

The Biggest Adult shrugs.

Snuffles turns and farts. *So much for you, too, fella.*

The humans pass several more cages. They don't reach in. The colors that swirl over their voices remind me of a storm cloud. It's all very confusing.

One of the puppies above me will be chosen. Last sunrise, there were nine puppies. This sunrise, there are five. The puppies go through the Good Side door quickly. I think it's because humans like to watch them grow. Humans place a lot of importance on growth, even when they have nothing to do with it.

The Biggest Adult, whose tag is Victor, I now know, stops and looks at them. *Hi, hi, hi!* The puppies yip. The Biggest Adult's mouth ticks up a tad, but the shadows on his face don't change. Interesting. This fellow doesn't like the taste of false enthusiasm, either.

I'm looking at his boots. Victor's boots. They are muddy and sturdy. I like hard work. Hard work is useful. Hard work is a full, round belly.

Victor squats. He groans as he does, a creaky old

door. But he's not old in his skin. His eyes narrow. He sees my torn left ear. No one wants me after they see my torn left ear. I tuck my head sideways so he doesn't have to look at it.

"That's Daisy," Janie says from behind her desk. Janie sits a lot. "She's a sweet thing, isn't she? About two years old, we think."

The boy, the one they labeled with the tag Micah, tilts his head at me. I know head tilts. Head tilts mean difficulties. "Her, Dad? I thought we were looking for a puppy."

Victor's eyes are deep like puddles. Puddles of sadness, not playful puddles. Tricky puddles, deep enough to drown in.

"That white spot around her eye looks like a daisy, see?" Janie says. "That's why we call her that. She's not the prettiest dog or the smartest dog, but she seems sweet."

Goodness, Janie. Manners? I am right here.

Victor slowly reaches in and scratches my jaw. "Hello, Miss Daisy."

Miss Daisy.

Miss.

I sit up.

At last, a human who understands the need for respect.

"Can I see her?" Mr. Victor asks. I decide to call him *Mr.* Victor, since he affords me the same respect.

The Awkward One steps forward. "I don't know, Victor," he says, lemon-sour words. "She's injured, and it looks like she's recently had pups. And don't forget, we only have ten weeks of training under the VA funding. If she can't be trained in two and a half months, well . . . she might not be our best choice."

"Dad, did you see these puppies?" Micah says.

Mr. Victor stands abruptly. "Her, please." His voice has snap, a flapping flag. "Can I see her?"

Janie unlocks my cage. Swings open the door.

I don't exit.

"See, Victor?" The Awkward One says. "I don't think she's right for you."

"Come, Miss Daisy," Mr. Victor says sternly. He pats his leg. His voice is full of pride, like a raw T-bone steak.

I walk out of the cage. Sit next to his sturdy, muddy boots. Watch to see what he wants me to do next.

Mr. Victor scratches me under the chin. I look up at him.

7

His smell is clean but bold, like fear and sweat. And his voice is difficult to read. It's a mixture of sunset and ghosts and blood. Something is missing from it, too. Something important.

I understand then.

This human doesn't want me.

This human *needs* me.

This is where I can prove how useful I am.

"We'll take her," Mr. Victor says.

Micah crams his hands in his pockets. He kicks the metal door on my cage, and it swings shut with a purple-bruise clang. "You said I could help pick! You never listen to what I want!"

Micah storms out the Good Side door. This time, the bell above it sounds red, like a warning.

★ 2 ★

LEASHES
AND OTHER INDIGNITIES

When the humans—my new pack members, it seems—open the car door, I jump in and sit in the seat next to Mr. Victor. I understand that he is the one who needs me, not Micah. But Micah frowns and says, "Nope. Into the backseat, Daisy." I hang my head and crawl into the cramped, dark back of the car. It smells like old milk.

Luckily, the journey home is glorious. The humans, Mr. Victor and Micah, open up the glass on the car as we ride in it. The air is spiced with autumn leaves and rain. It is such a different scent from the desperation and loneliness I was used to smelling at the shelter. I can't resist sticking my head outside as we speed along, even though it isn't very dignified of me. I even allow my tongue to loll about a time or two, when the humans aren't looking. *Lollolllllollllolll.* Slobber isn't respectable, but it usually signals fun.

Micah sees me. Grins. Sticks his head out the window, too.

Is he making fun of me? I pull my head inside. He pouts like a lemon and does, too.

When we reach the humans' home, Mr. Victor tugs on the leash that the Awkward One, tagged Alex, hung around my neck. I follow Mr. Victor inside. I have no choice, because I AM ON A GODFORSAKEN LEASH.

Leashes. They go against everything a civilized dog stands for. They are an indignity.

Inside, an Adult Female with a Crying Baby on her hip stubs out a cigarette. "Oh! You're home already! That was fast." The smell of cigarettes feels like long-ago burns on my skin from a horrible human. I decide to withhold judgment on this person, but it's not looking good. I hope she's not like my first pack.

"Anna," Mr. Victor says, his voice sharp knives. "You were smoking around the baby again."

Anna tosses her hair. The shadows on her face shift into defiance. She leans toward Mr. Victor to give him a kiss. He turns away.

Anna sighs. Stoops over me. "And you are?" Her voice is hard to picture. It disappears quickly.

"This is Miss Daisy," Mr. Victor says. I sit a little taller, because one should always strive to make a good first impression. Even if Anna's was less than stellar.

The Baby cries like metal cars crunching together. It is hard to listen to anything other than that.

Mr. Victor's face twitches. He notices, too.

"You're a gator pit," Anna says to me over the crying. Her face softens a bit. And her voice. Anna's. It's steam. There and gone.

"A what?" Micah asks. He looks at me as if I'm a surprise slice of bacon.

"A gator pit. A pit bull mix. My *abuelo* used to raise them. The brindle color, the bow legs, the pointed jaw, the big head . . ."

Pardon me?

". . . she's a prize one, this girl. My grandfather would've loved her."

The thing about steam? It's warm and clean, if temporary. I lift my nose. *Prize.* I like that.

11

Mr. Victor drops the leash. I take this as my invitation to explore.

There are cardboard boxes everywhere. They smell like another place, one far from here, with different trees and foreign dirt. I wonder if one of the boxes will be my bed. Cardboard isn't very comfortable, but with the right garbage inside, a box can be pleasant.

The one tagged Anna watches me, her face shadows shifting into worry. Worry smells like too-old meat. "I just don't know, Victor," she says, bouncing the crying baby on her hip. "One more thing to take care of? And the money . . ."

"The dog is paid for by the VA. I told you. Training for ten weeks, then everything else after that, if she passes her tests."

That sounds horrible: *tests*. It sounds like poking and prodding.

"*If* she passes?" Anna looks at me like I'm a floating fish.

"She'll pass."

"Yeah, but the food and the vet bills."

"Anna, my therapist says this is the best thing for PTSD." Mr. Victor's voice sounds growly, and my own neck hairs prickle at it. If he's on the defense, so am I. I know to protect the alpha dog. "Do you want me to work on this or not?"

Out of the corner of my eye, I see Micah's face shadows shift into worry, too. He looks at me like a small green bud poking through the soil in spring.

I lower my nose to the worn, stained carpet and sniff deeply.

It doesn't smell like these humans. This pack. My pack.

I sniff around some more. No, these humans are definitely new here. In this den.

There is also . . . *something*. A fishy, scaly something nearby. Perhaps these humans had tuna for dinner.

A few more sniffs and, yep! Just as I suspected. The other humans who were here before had a dog. A dachshund. Twelve years old. With a bladder infection.

This pack doesn't seem at all concerned that the other pack could return, try to reclaim this den. I need to make certain that dachshund knows my pack lives here now.

I know what needs to be done. I need to take drastic measures. I wouldn't normally do this, here, but pack dynamics are everything. And I need to prove myself useful to this new pack.

I squat.

I mark our territory. My new pack will be so happy to know I'm protecting us right away!

"Gross! Miss Daisy's peeing!" Micah yells, his voice like a whack from a broomstick. He points at me. I'm embarrassed. Embarrassment tastes like raisins on an otherwise great pizza.

"Daisy!" Anna snaps. Her face shadows fall into a scowl. She doesn't call me *Miss*. I tuck my tail.

Mr. Victor droops into a chair with a heavy sigh. His scent and his colors confuse me.

"We'll see, okay, guys?" he says. "We'll see. And if she doesn't work out, we'll find a different dog."

A *different dog*.

He didn't say *another* dog.

He said a *different* dog.

I understand the difference.

Mr. Victor and Anna and Micah forget I'm here. They go away separately. I decide to work on freeing myself from the leash, because I cannot tolerate such tyranny. The leash is leather, so not unpleasant to chew. It's nice and gummy when Anna spots me.

"Daisy! Don't chew your leash. Do you want me

to take it off?" She crosses to me. My tail thumps. I'm usually not so dependent on humans, but leashes are an evil that requires thumbed assistance.

Mr. Victor snaps awake from his chair. "Don't do that, Anna." He groans to standing and grabs the stick he uses to walk. I don't like sticks, but Mr. Victor doesn't swing this one like some other sticks I've seen.

"Do what?" Anna says, her voice melting away.

"Take the leash off," Micah yells from the other room. I can't see him, but I can hear the shade in his voice. It's anger, like red poison berries. Red is the color of things that burn and scar. Janie at the shelter used to tell people that dogs can't see colors, but that's not true. Colors are the tint of your instincts.

Micah appears in the doorway. "Alex says the leash has to stay on for thirty days," he continues. "And no one but Dad can walk the dog, or let the dog out, or feed the dog, or even pet the thing."

Thing? I sniff.

"What?" Anna says with a snort-laugh. "She has to wear a leash all the time?"

My heartbeat speeds. I look to Mr. Victor for confirmation of this horrible news.

"It's only for thirty days." This statement is a thorn.

15

"And we can't *pet her*?" Anna looks at me with so much pity, I begin to wonder what I've gotten myself into with this pack.

"Alex says it will build a bond between us," Mr. Victor says, "if I'm the only one who interacts with her."

Micah rolls his eyes. "Only the *handler*—that's Dad—can do those things. *All good things must come from the handler.* Alex the dog trainer said that. So much for getting a pet." He sighs, and it feels like a knife slice.

If I'm not a pet, what am I?

"C'mon, Miss Daisy." Mr. Victor says. "I'll take you for a—*ew*. Gross," he says, grabbing my slobbery leash. "Anna, will you hand me a—"

But Anna has already walked away. She is steam.

Mr. Victor sighs and grabs a paper towel. He also plucks a bright red fruit off a small tree in the kitchen.

When we get outside, I want to *run*, but I can't, because I AM ATTACHED TO A GODFORSAKEN LEASH. I pull against it. My muscles are strong and I think I can break it if I keep trying. Mr. Victor will be proud of my strength if I can break through this thing.

"Stop that!" Mr. Victor says with a yank. His order

is like walking on gravel. He snaps open the fruit and rubs it up and down the length of the leather. "This pepper will stop that chewing of yours."

But I'm too panicked to try and puzzle out what that means because *I AM ATTACHED TO A GODFORSAKEN LEASH!* Thirty days of this? I will surely die a slow, graceless death, tied up like an animal. I grab the leather between my teeth and—

OH!

OH! HOT HOT FIRE HOT OH!

My tongue burns.

My nose burns.

My whole head burns.

I rub my paws over my face.

I drag my tongue and jaws across the grass.

I sneeze.

I sneeze again.

I tug Mr. Victor over to a puddle and I lap up water.

And then I stop.

Because above me, Mr. Victor's face shadows slowly shift to point up, not down. He's wheezing. His heart beats rapidly.

Is something wrong? Is he broken?

And then he bares his teeth.

My interaction with humans has been limited to one pack, but I do know that when a human bares his teeth, it isn't a sign of aggression. No, for humans, showing teeth means yellow sunshine joy. It is a *smile*.

And Mr. Victor is awkward at it, this smiling thing. His shadows curve at unused angles. This expression of his is dusty. It occurs to me that it is the first time I've seen him do it. It's the first time I've seen anyone in this pack do it. Even not-a-pet Micah, who now peers out the window, is scowling.

Come to think of it, this entire pack of humans is bad at it. Bad at smiling.

I vow to change that. This pack needs more yellow sunshine joy.

★ 3 ★

INSTINCT IS
YOUR BONES KNOWING

My new pack is tagged "the Abeyta family." Last night they gave me a pillow to sleep on next to Mr. Victor. A pillow! Like I'm royalty or something. And I don't wish to sound spoiled, but the pillow was enjoyable. I forgive them for this silly luxury, though, because they also made me wear the leash while I slept.

When I wake with the next sunrise, I stretch, squeal, smack my jaws. Anna winks at me. It worries me. I hope her eye is okay. Eye health is very important for survival.

Mr. Victor and Micah and I ride in the glorious car again. I stick my head out the window and smell crisp burning leaves and bright yellow sunshine and deep, rich, diggable dirt. My fur tinkles like chimes in the wind. I decide that if I could pick one thing to do for the rest of my life, it would be to ride in a car and smell the world.

We stop at a building that has no windows and the scent of a thousand dogs. Dreadful. Inside, the white floor is cold on my foot pads and makes my toenails click, the sound like raindrops on a metal Dumpster roof. It's a sound full of concern. I worry that at this new place, I'll be put in a cage again. I pull on the leash because if there's one thing worse than leashes, it's cages.

But inside, the Awkward One tagged Alex is there. He looks at Micah. "Hey, bud." His eyes slide to Mr. Victor. "It's more effective if you train Daisy alone, you know. Having two of you here confuses her."

I purse my lips. *Is that so?* There is no doubt in my mind that Micah isn't the one I answer to. He hasn't even looked at me since yesterday's scowl, and his voice is undrinkable water, like foamy puddles on the beach. He is not mine, and I am not his, and if it weren't for the fact that he arrived in my pack before me, I'd question his usefulness.

"I'm the one training her," Mr. Victor says. Micah shrugs into a colorful thing that covers his ears. The thing has wires coming out of it that plug into the plastic box he holds. How dangerous it is, to block your hearing like that! I pull toward him to warn him, but Mr. Victor is gripping the leash. Micah sulks into a corner and pushes buttons on the box with his thumbs.

"Okay, so." Alex the Awkward claps his hands. The sound makes me jump because it echoes in this large, empty room like a metal truck rattling over a pothole. Alex squints at me. I squint at him.

"Today we're going to evaluate Daisy here using the SAFER assessment," Alex says. He taps a clipboard, and I imagine small bursts of orange sparking off it. "This'll let us see if she has the right temperament to be a service dog."

Alex knots his fingers together. "I should let you know, Victor, that there is no such thing as passing or failing a temperament test."

Whew. I can't fail.

"However, only about ten percent of dogs have

the right temperament to become a service dog. And of *those*, only about thirty percent can actually pass the certification test."

Humans. They put so much stock in their numbers. There is much more to be said for instinct. Instinct is your bones knowing.

"So . . ." Alex's forehead lumps. "Odds are against your Daisy, here."

That Alex is a real thorn. His voice is the same color green as when I eat too much grass and throw up. And today he smells like burps.

Alex drags out a clear box full of things. "What we're looking for is a biddable dog. Easy to handle, eager to please. Soft. Mushy."

I am neither soft nor mushy, thank you. I vow to stop sleeping on pillows. People are getting the wrong impression.

"If this assessment shows those qualities," Alex continues, ignoring me, "I'll recommend that she go forward with the training."

"And if she doesn't?" Mr. Victor says, handing my leash over to Alex.

Alex shrugs. His apathy for my future tastes like seaweed. "We can't waste time on an untrainable dog,

Victor. Or money. Ten weeks. That's all we've got."
He snaps my leash. I shrink.

Untrainable? Sounds messy. Like fluff ripped
from a cheap toy.

"I'll walk her through this initial assessment, but
that's the only time someone other than you should
handle Daisy," Alex says. At that, Micah's heart races.
I can hear the squeak of his teeth clenching together,
a sharp crack in the pavement.

Does he want me to fail?

Mr. Victor kneels next to me, rubs my neck. "You
hear that, Miss Daisy?" he says, leaning toward my
injured ear. "Show him your best, girl."

I promise, Mr. Victor.

"Ah-ah-ah!" Alex says, yanking the leash backward. It surprises me and pulls me away from Mr.
Victor. "The number one rule with dogs, Victor:
always protect your face."

*The number one rule with humans, Alex: always
protect your pack.*

Alex walks me across the room. I don't like walking away from my pack—I can't protect them from
across this big, smelly space. I pull against the leash.
Alex isn't my pack. I'm supposed to be with them.

23

Alex clicks his tongue. "She's not doing well with restraint. Her reaction to this leash isn't positive."

Of course it's not. Shall I retrieve a leash for you, fella?

The shadows on Mr. Victor's face darken. They are green on the edges, showing worry. *Oh no.*

I try to relax. I huff. *Sorry I wanted to put you on a leash, Alex.*

We walk a few laps around the room and stop. Alex nods. "Not too bad, Daisy, once you got used to it." He starts petting me, then pulling at my skin and legs, each tug not unpleasant. I enjoy the massage until he gets to my injured ear. When he reaches for that, I stiffen and purse my lips. The hairs on my back rise.

"Hmmm," Alex says. "Her reaction to touch is overall fine. But she protects that ear, even though it's healed."

No one touches that ear. No one.

Mr. Victor's face shadows pull farther down. *Poo.* Micah's, on the other hand, lighten a tad. *Double poo.*

I'm going to fail this test. They said I couldn't fail, but I will. I'll be the first. Mortifying.

Will I go back to a cage?

I don't like toy lightning.

I have to try harder.

Alex starts jogging with the leash, so I trot to keep up. He bobs and weaves, so I do, too. He jumps, shouts, claps. The sounds he makes are like walking through spiderwebs: confusing and sticky. I watch him calmly, trying to read clues if I'm supposed to react to this silliness.

"Good, Daisy," Alex says. To Mr. Victor, he says, "She's fine with new experiences, like movement and sound."

Mr. Victor's shadows lighten a bit. I smile. Micah shifts like he's uncomfortable. Can no one else hear his teeth grinding? He's going to break a tooth soon.

Alex pulls out this huge pillowy thing that, when you look at it from the right angle, might resemble a human arm. Alex pokes me with the thing. Do they think I cannot tell the difference between a fake arm and a real one? I am very confused but I let him poke me with it. It smells like it's poked ten thousand other dogs. Disgusting. Alex needs to invest in some cleaning solutions.

"She doesn't tend toward biting, which is excellent," Alex says. I can smell Mr. Victor's pride from across the room, a beefy, bloody pride. I've never been a fighter, so I'm happy that biting isn't something this pack needs. *Excellent, indeed.*

Alex the Awkward digs a bunch of stuff out of the clear box and tosses things around the room. He then walks me through the things. One of the things is a toy that quacks like a duck every few moments, spurting off bursts of purple. Annoying, but certainly avoidable. Another thing is a bacon treat. My mouth waters when we approach it, but I get the feeling I'm supposed to ignore it, based on the tension in the leash.

"Nice job, Daisy," Alex says. He turns to Mr. Victor. "Okay, last assessment. Let's bring her into the next room to meet other dogs."

Mr. Victor's heart speeds. His shadows darken again. "Other dogs . . . other people?"

Alex softens his hold on the leash. I can tell he likes and respects Mr. Victor. It's the only reason why Alex is tolerable, really. "They're all veterans, too, Colonel. You'll be fine."

Colonel?

I can tell right away, by the taste of this word, that this is an important tag: *colonel*. It sounds like "kernel," like airy popcorn, but it tastes like fine meaty sausage. Like a tag that Mr. Victor worked very hard to earn. It is useful. *He* is useful. I resolve to call him *Colonel* instead of *Mister*. I am mortified that I didn't do so earlier.

The Colonel and Micah and Alex and I cross the hallway into a new room. A group of six dogs and their handlers is gathered. Colonel Victor's shadows flush a worrisome deep gray the moment we're around other humans who aren't in our pack. His heart quickens. He begins to sweat.

Strangers make him as nervous as they make me.

Micah seems to sense this. He slides his hand into the Colonel's. The Colonel grips it, hard, but Micah doesn't wince.

Strong boy. Good instincts.

Alex walks me into the room and past each dog.

Guten tag, says a German shepherd mix when I trot by.

Hello.

A full-breed golden retriever is next. She doesn't even sniff in my direction. She shakes her gorgeous glossy mane. I decide to ignore her, too. Snob.

Next is a Great Dane—*Hello, down there*—then a Lab mix—*Howdy-do*—and then a standard poodle—*Bonjour.* Typical.

Finally, a wiry-haired mutt who smells like beef

27

treats leaps out at me. *Hi, doll! Watch this! If I wrap around you, and you go over there . . . good! yes! Our leashes will get all tangled, and the humans will have to dance like puppets to unravel themselves. Watch! Ha-HA! DANCE, PUPPETS! That's what you get for putting ol' Hawkeye on a leash!*

Sure enough, Alex and the other human throw an arm here, a leg there, and are forced to twist and turn to balance themselves. "Whoa! Easy there, Hawkeye!" "Daisy! Steady!" Micah giggles at these shenanigans, small dandelions of laughter.

Hawkeye takes a long and somewhat invasive sniff of me, then gives me a sloppy wet nudge with his nose. *Thanks, doll. I always get a kick out of making the humans do that.*

Any other time, I think I'd enjoy these games. I'm not against fun. But I know today is important to Colonel Victor. I narrow my eyes at the mutt. *It's Daisy, not doll, you pig. And if you just made me fail this test, I'll hunt you down and nip you in unpleasant places. Doll.* I nudge him back.

He laughs. *Call me!* He jangles the tag around his neck that lists his human's telephone number.

Back in the other room, Alex says, "Hmmm," and, "Mmmhmmm," while checking things on a piece

28

of paper. His utterances sound like, well, there's no other way to put this: *bathroom* noises. He slides his pen behind his ear, his mouth pursed to one side of his face. His expression reminds me of a hot dog: you're never *quite sure* what you're getting.

"Victor, Daisy here is what I'd call right on the line."

"You mean she passed?" Colonel Victor lifts his chin at me, and my chest puffs with pride. I enjoy a squirrel-chasing thrill. Micah's heartbeat flares.

Hope or disappointment? Hard to tell. Why are my instincts so murky with that one?

"No—there is no pass or fail," Alex says. *Killjoy.* "She scored well in many areas, but not in others, at least with regard to the temperament of a service dog. I'm torn. And because this training is so rigorous and, well, so expensive, when I'm torn, my recommendation is no."

No.

Alex continues: "The money you've received only pays for ten weeks of training. I worry that a dog like Daisy"—the way he says my name makes me picture a pile of writhing worms—"can't be trained before the money runs out. You'd have to pay for her training past that."

"Well, that's impossible," the Colonel cuts in. His face shadows are still murky and distrustful after being around other humans who aren't in our pack. He kneels beside me, grunting like rips of fabric. He lifts his tinted glasses to look me in the eyes.

"Can you do this, Miss Daisy?"

I'm still not whole-hog certain I understand what "this" is. I know it means I must be useful. But how? A service dog isn't a pet, it seems. But I've already failed at being a pet once.

I think so.

"Are you sure you don't want a full-breed dog, Victor?" Alex asks. "They can be much easier to train, and the assistance is still available. I think it'd be a smarter use of the money."

"No. I want a rescue dog," Colonel Victor says, his gaze not leaving mine. His eyes are soft; his voice, like sand. We live near sand. I know that sand can build things up or wear things down. "I like the idea of rescue." His pupils are wide, but his breathing is calm.

"Can you *do this*, Miss Daisy?" he whispers again. "I need . . ." His words trail off like a lost scent.

I straighten my back, my tail. Lift my chin.

I can.

Colonel Victor stands with a groan. "I'm sticking with Miss Daisy."

Micah's thumbs slam against his plastic toy, small firecrackers of anger exploding.

Disappointment from the boy.

A pet, I am not.

And now I've made a promise I hope I can keep.

★ 4 ★

IT'S A HUMAN'S WORLD

The ride home isn't glorious. My pack forgets to roll down the window, and we're missing all the best smells, like the hot dog stand and the squishy, splashy mud puddles and the statue where the seagulls poo. I need to learn how to do it myself: roll down the windows.

Micah slumps in the front seat, his head leaning against the glass. Those big, puffy plastic things still cover his ears. That kid is really trying to get doom's attention, wearing those. What if a bear attacks?

I pace the backseat, window to window, hoping

one of them will magically open for me. I scratch at the glass with my paw. Whining sometimes helps open things, too, so I throw that in. Things just somehow OPEN for humans. It's a human's world. Maybe if I just keep trying. *Nope. Let's try that one. Nope. Let's try this one. Nope. Let's try that one. Nope. Let's try this one. . . .*

"Daisy, cut it out," Micah says over his shoulder. An icicle.

I slump onto my seat, too.

The car is quiet for a moment, then:

Tweee.

My head cocks to the side. It's a small, high-pitched sound. Orange and annoying, a piece of food caught in my teeth.

Micah adjusts in his seat. His scent changes briefly from stagnant to ripples.

TweeeTWEEEE.

Micah pulls off his ear coverings.

"Dad! Dad, listen!" He puckers his lips.

TweeTweeTweeTWEEEE.

"I learned to whistle!"

TweeTweetTweedle.

The whistle makes me cringe because it is a toothache. My head cocks to the other side. Whistling is so high-pitched. It is involuntary, my head twisting like this, and it's very, very annoying.

TweeTweeTWEEETwee.

Colonel Victor shudders. I hear, under the sound of the bothersome tweeing, Colonel Victor's heartbeat speed up. His breathing speeds, too, and he begins panting, like when I'm too hot. He is seeing white. I can feel the white growing inside his head.

Why isn't Micah helping him?

TweeTWEEEE.

The car swerves. I fall over. Colonel Victor smells strongly of fear, a dark house full of nails and teeth.

"Dad?"

Help him, Micah! Be useful!

The car veers, and another car honks red at us. It's hard for me to stand on the swerving seat, but I do. I reach forward and nudge Colonel Victor on his bare arm with my cold, wet nose.

His shadows lighten slightly. Dark gray, like ash.

"Daisy, stop!" Micah yells. "Dad?"

I keep nudging him. My bones tell me he can't remember where he is. The car scrapes against the side rail of the highway, the sound of puppies crying.

Wake up, Colonel. Wake up now. I push him as hard as I can with the top of my head. *Colonel!*

"Daisy, cut it out!" Micah shouts at me.

Colonel Victor's hammering heart slows a bit. He shivers. Spits out a word as sharp as a tack.

He swings the car to the side of the road. Stops the engine. Puts his head back and closes his eyes. His breathing is thin smoke, his heart quivering. But he's returning to *now*. I can feel him coming back.

"Dad, are you okay?"

Colonel Victor ignores Micah's question and turns to me. The blacks of his eyes are still wide, but I can tell he can focus now. He is no longer away.

"You know, don't you, Miss Daisy?" he asks. His voice vibrates like a gunshot. He grabs the muzzle of my neck and pulls me close to him. He buries his face in my fur. He smells like the dogs who went through the Bad Side door. He's crying, and he doesn't want Micah to see, so I wedge myself further between them. Micah flushes hot at that.

The Colonel's shadows turn to thin pale red lines. His heart slows. "Thank you. I knew you were the right pick, Miss Daisy. Thank you."

I'm not sure what I've done, other than pull him back from straying away. Any dog would do that for a pack member.

We sit like that for a minute, with him hugging

35

me. His tears soak into my fur. Micah is crying, too, his tears tiny oceans. He is not getting hugged. I can feel him feeling that—NOT hugged.

Colonel Victor snaps straight.

"No more whistling, Micah."

"What? But I—"

"No more."

When we get home, Micah slams the door to his den—*bam!*—the sound of a kick in the ribs. Colonel Victor winces but is otherwise fine.

The woman, Anna, and the baby aren't here. I sniff around a bit, still trying to find the source of the fishy smell. It's lingered for days. Yesterday I even poked around in the garbage, which says a lot, because garbage smells like loss and good-bye. But I didn't find it because Anna yelled red sirens at me.

Tick-tick-tick-SWISH. Approaching: small clicking noises, then the sound of something heavy being dragged across the floor. Like small splinters of chopped wood, then the tree cracking and falling. And again: *tick-tick-tick-SWISH.*

I open my nostrils and sniff.

Fish scales.

Around the corner he lopes, long toenails ticking

on the floor. It's a lizard, a huge one, about the size of a small cat, with spikes jutting forth from his chin and down his back. He is beyond ugly; he is plastic litter. I scramble to my feet. The hair on my back barbs, and I taste unknown things.

Relax, grasshopper, says the lizard. One of his eyes rolls skyward, but the other one stays firmly locked on me. Creepy, like spaghetti snakes. I've always distrusted spaghetti. *I am here, too,* the thing says. *I am Smaug, dragon healer of precious things.*

I take a step backward. Smaug takes a step forward. The tail on this lizard is several inches long and whips across the floor dully—the sound from before, of the tree falling. It appears as if his tail has a life of its own, as if it's fighting for freedom from Smaug.

I am in Micah's room, Smaug says, *when I do not wish to explore. A word of warning: those who do not enter frequently become unwelcome entirely.*

Excuse me? I've never been in Micah's room. There's never been a purpose for me in there. Why would I do something with no purpose? Purpose is everything.

Smaug sizes me up, his odd eyeballs twitching, his tongue darting to and fro. *You have much to learn about loyalty.*

I snuff. *I beg your pardon. You have much to learn about not talking like a fortune cookie.*

Shuffling sounds come from Colonel Victor's chair. Smaug turns. *Here is where I leave you. I do not wish to end this journey just yet.*

Tick-tick-tick-SWISH—splinters and fallen trees— Smaug waddles away, around the corner, his long, long tail snapping out of sight just as the Colonel stands.

I see that lizard's game. The big humans don't know he wanders the house.

Colonel Victor limps into the kitchen and opens a bunch of bottles. The pills he pours into his hand are blue and red and pink and make me think of howling sad songs. He tosses them into his mouth and gulps water. Soon, his heart slows even more, to a dull, unnatural thud. His face lines turn foggy, changing to a cool off-white color—not his normal shade. It's an artificial color for him, like light from a bulb instead of the sun.

Loud music pounds from Micah's den—*boom, boom, boom*—a herd of stomping rats in a sewer.

Colonel Victor slumps into his chair. He taps his leg for me to sit next to him, so I do. But then he taps his leg again. I realize he's asking me to jump into his lap. I do.

I fit perfectly—my front paws hanging off one arm of the chair, my back legs off the other, my tail directly in Colonel Victor's face. He dusts off a rare grin through the fog.

"Thank you for earlier, Miss Daisy."

You're welcome.

I'm unsure why it was important. I did what any pack member would do. Any pack member but Micah, apparently.

He sighs and picks at the fabric on his chair. "Driving is dangerous now, too. I can't do any of the things I used to love. Hunting, fishing." He tilts his face around to look in my eyes, and his voice is suddenly a raccoon lying too still in the middle of the highway. "But you don't want to hear any of this, do you?"

Go ahead.

"I fight with my wife. I fight with my son. I can barely hold the baby . . ."

His voice turns twitchy, a too-late jolt of the raccoon's tail. He finds a string on the chair and pulls it.

You can tell me.

"They say I'm 'unemployable.' I mean, that's the definition of a *service*man—service. And now I'm useless? It's the ultimate insult."

My whole self softens. Yes. I understand. Useless-ness is the highest dishonor. It is the ultimate cone of shame.

I have been called useless.

But he's wrong. Colonel Victor is not useless. He's the alpha dog of this pack. He must still be confused.

His eyes turn watery. He tries to swallow it back, but I can hear the knot in his throat.

"I can't turn it off, Miss Daisy. The constant seek-ing and searching for danger. I can't turn it off."

He's crying now. He's bad at it, too. He chokes and gasps like red raccoon guts spilled on pavement. I can tell he doesn't let himself cry a lot. He pulls the string from his chair and it gets longer.

"That's why I told Micah not to whistle. It sounds too much like incoming mortar shells. The sound I heard before my friends . . ."

The string he pulls pops. Colonel Victor sobs but tries to clench it in his throat like a fist. Tears make rivers on his face.

I shift on his lap and reach up. I give him a quick kiss on the cheek. I catch a tear on my tongue. It tastes like fighting a bigger dog. I never wanted to do that—fight the bigger dog. Fight any dog.

He thumps my rib cage in thanks. We are a team,

and I think of wet-nosed nuzzles from my family.

"They keep calling me a wounded warrior, Miss Daisy. But I don't feel like either of those—wounded or a warrior. If I were a warrior, I would've brought every man back home." His voice cracks like gunfire.

I don't know what that means, exactly, but I know he is a warrior. The essence of it is written on his soul.

"And wounded? I guess. But I actually just feel . . ."

He pauses to think of the word, and his fingers pick at another string on his chair. My ears perk toward the hallway. Micah is just around the corner, listening. His shade bleeds around the door frame: a murky horizon, like a dark, sad, gray ocean on a rainy day. I can hear the tears on his cheeks.

"Broken. I feel broken."

★ 5 ★

THE DIFFERENCE BETWEEN
SMART AND OBEDIENT

"**O**kay, so . . ." Alex the Awkward claps his hands. I have lived with the Abeyta pack now for seven sunrises, and I've seen Alex every insufferable day. So his hand-clapping doesn't make me jump anymore because I know that's what Alex does to make himself sound Important: he claps. I understand the need to feel Important. Important tastes like beef gravy.

But when Alex claps, his scent wafts off him, and that's a problem because he smells bad. This human bathes in onions, I believe. And today, even his voice has that yellowy-green tint to it that makes me taste wild onions. I gag a bit, and Alex squints at me.

He thinks I'm gagging because I'm still protesting the leash. Which I'm not. I don't *love* the leash, don't get me wrong. It's still an abomination. But I enjoy the connection it gives me to Colonel Victor. It's a tendon that joins us, and I can read him better when he's holding it. When he tenses, I feel it through the leash as sure as salt.

When Micah tenses, I feel nothing. It happens a lot. He wears tense all the way from the crease in his forehead to the toes of his sneakers, which drag when he walks. His tense feels different from the Colonel's, and even Alex's. His tense feels like he's rooting for me to fail. I don't know why.

"We're doing one more training day in here"— Alex sweeps his hands wide, as if this plain white building were a palace—"before we take our training into the real world."

Those two words—*real world*—make sparks burn across the shades of Colonel Victor's face and turn them to ash. But he nods. He's brave, my alpha dog.

"So I think Daisy's ready for this." Alex holds up a piece of cloth, the color of sand. "This is your vest, Daisy," he squeaks at me in a high-pitched tone. This voice of his—the one he uses only for me—is like chewy, sticky caramel. "VEST. You'll wear it when you work. It's your UNIFORM."

He shouts those two words, but I look past his stupidity because I understand: these are my working clothes! Like the Colonel's muddy boots. Talk about Important! This is chuck roast beef gravy. This says *I AM USEFUL*.

"Do you want a VEST, girl? Do you?"

I've only tasted caramel once, in the Dumpster behind the ice cream parlor where I used to live. The humans there threw away a whole tub just because a tiny cockroach climbed inside for a swim—so wasteful! I ate so much of it I threw up. Deliciously sickening.

That is my now: I know Alex is squeaking to be sweet, but it's too big. His sweet is overwhelming, like eating an entire tub of caramel instead of a dollop.

"VEST, girl! But first, Daisy needs to go to the bathroom." Alex opens the one door that leads outside, and the air out there smells of water in sandy soil and lush grass and palm trees swishing. "Once she's wearing her vest, there is no going to the bathroom. Ever. No eating, either. When she's wearing the vest, she's on the clock. Working. Okay, Victor?"

"Got it."

"Daisy!" Alex says, his voice raising to a sticky-sweet pitch again. It's so annoying, getting squeaked at like this. Why does he only talk to me in that voice? Micah is also a lower-ranked pack member, and he gets a normal taupe tone. "C'mon, Daisy! Do your business!"

Seriously? Do your business? I look up at Colonel Victor.

But the Colonel just leads me to the door. "Stay here, Micah," he says to the corner. Micah nods, even though his ears are covered again. I worry about whether he's endangering our pack with those things. Surely he cannot protect himself, and those who cannot protect themselves are the spoiled link in the sausages.

"Do your business, Daisy!" Alex screeches, and I want to lick my teeth just listening to him. He looks at me and dangles my vest in front of me like a bribe. "Do your business and we'll put on your VEST."

I snuff. I want that vest and apparently I have to poop to get it. So I do. Ridiculous. And they give me *no* privacy. Appalling.

"Good *girl*, Daisy!" Alex squeals.

I've never seen anyone so excited to watch a dog use the restroom. I finish and scratch the grass, because I'm no savage. Alex scoops it up with a plastic bag. It's every proof I need that he is indeed insane.

Back inside, Colonel Victor straps on my vest. I feel I might pop open the straps of the thing, my chest puffs so full of filet mignon pride.

"You look great, Miss Daisy," the Colonel says.

Thank you. I do look smashing, don't I?

"Great," Alex says, and claps again. I try not to gag at the cloud of onion gas it propels my way, but I don't succeed. Alex squints at me. "Last week's training was getting Daisy acquainted with the basics: Sit. Stay. Come."

Easy-peasy. Nailed it.

"Today we're going to teach some additional obedience commands and address any behavioral issues we might have while learning those. From there, we'll develop short-term and long-term goals for you and Daisy here."

Colonel Victor nods. He smells like impatience. Alex talks these same words every day.

"The training from this point is hard work, Victor," Alex continues. "That's why we train daily.

And we only have nine weeks left, so we really need to buckle down. It requires repetition, consistency, compassion, timing, and a ton of patience."

"With you or with the dog?" Colonel Victor asks.

Alex stops talking. His face blushes with hot-sauce embarrassment.

The Colonel winks his eye whiskers. "C'mon, I was teasing, Alex. I'm used to hard work. Let's get started."

Alex takes a deep breath and his shadows cool a bit. He jogs across the room to another clear plastic bin.

"Okay, Daisy," he squeaks. "Let's learn some new words."

"BALL," he squeak-shouts, and he holds up a ball. The caramel taste flares again from my belly. He places the ball back in the bin.

Oh, heavens.

"SOCK." Alex holds up a sock. He returns the sock to the bin.

Really? I look at Colonel Victor. He's not tensing up at this idiocy, though, so I try to let it slide.

"TOY."

"BONE."

"STICK."

I purse my lips. *C'mon.*

Alex jogs back to us. He unclips my leash—*hallelujah!*—and squeals, "GO GET THE SOCK, DAISY. THE SOCK. GO GET IT. THE SOCK. THE SOCK. SOCK, DAISY!"

I snuff. I trot to the box, nose through its contents, retrieve the sock, and bring it back.

"GOOD GIRL, DAISY! EXCELLENT! OH, WHAT A SMART GIRL YOU ARE."

I am underemployed, is what I am.

"BALL, DAISY! WHERE'S YOUR BALL? GET THE BALL! BALL, GIRL! BALL. BALL. BALL!"

I do as I'm asked. I get the ball out of the box. The glory that is heaped upon me is whipped-cream-with-sprinkles incredulous.

"STICK, DAISY! WHICH ONE IS THE STICK? GET THE STICK, GIRL. STICK!"

I roll my eyes and get the stick, already. I drop it at his feet. *Seriously, Alex. Challenge me here.*

"BONE, DAISY! GO GET THE BONE, GIRL. WHICH ONE IS THE BONE?"

Enough already.

I jog to the box, clamp my teeth around the handle, and drag the whole thing back.

There. There's everything you could possibly need, Alex.

Alex's forehead crinkles like paper. His face darkens with green worry lines.

Uh-oh. I look up to Colonel Victor.

The Colonel's heartbeat skips and his shoulders start shaking.

Big *uh-oh.* What have I done? Have I pushed him too far? Alex calls this *out of sync*—have I pushed the Colonel out of sync? Oh my.

But instead, the Colonel snorts. He bottom-of-his belly, bend-over laughs. He flares like a bonfire with each guffaw.

"She outsmarted you, Alex," Colonel Victor said. "She brought you the whole box!"

Alex shakes his head. "I don't know. I think it's a sign of behavioral issues—"

But the Colonel keeps chuckling, and his bright red laughter burns away some of the shadows that color him always. He ruffles the fur on my head. I smile, relaxing my jaw and letting my tongue loll out. Even Micah, who sits in the corner, ears covered, giggles little hiccups of green-and-yellow joy. My tail thumps because I've pleased my pack.

"I think it could be a serious issue. . . ." Alex is saying, but none of us are listening to his useless cat litter words.

When we finally calm ourselves, Colonel Victor sighs like wind. "She's a smart dog, Alex. She got those items first thing."

Alex's shoulders drop. "She's smart, yes. But she's stubborn. She disobeyed. There's a difference between a smart dog and an obedient dog, and for this job, we need an obedient dog."

The Colonel tightens his grip on the leash. The lights behind his face cool, a setting sun. So do Micah's. I've disappointed them. Disappointment tastes like earthworms.

I tuck my tail. Why did I go and show off like that?

They'll send me back to the shelter.

Alex digs in his pocket. He bends and looks me in the eye.

"These are service dog patches, Daisy," he says, holding up tiny round pieces of colorful cloth. He doesn't squeak. His voice is dog-treat serious. I pay attention.

"You have your vest," he says, and points to my uniform. "If you pass your service dog test, Victor will sew these patches on your vest. Then you'll be a true elite. A real service dog. I want you to be an elite dog, Daisy. I want you to earn these patches. We have nine weeks, Daisy. Nine."

He tucks the delicious patches back into his pocket.

An elite.

The Colonel's grip on the leash tightened when he heard that word, so I understand.

An elite is Important. It's special, unique, different from just *pet*. It's a tasty word, like chicken. Elite is useful.

I was told I was useless by the other humans, my first pack, and then they left me in a Dumpster. I'll do everything I can, toenails to tail tip, to be the opposite of useless.

I want those patches so much I can feel it down to my paw pads.

Elite.

★ 6 ★

DON'T FLY, DAISY

When ten Micahs are turned loose in a big room, they run and scream and whack one another with plastic sticks, and it's like being caught on the beach in a sudden storm: sound and sand and salt pelting you from all around. Stinging everywhere. But oddly happy. The boys don't seem miserable. Just the opposite: they bare their teeth and whoop and climb things and jump off things and *fly* to the ground, and whoa, does flying ever look like fun.

But I'm not here to have fun. This is a birthday party, after all. I'm on the job.

Sit, I remind myself as I stay seated next to Colonel Victor. I practice my commands even when the rest of my pack doesn't. It helps me be more useful. Elite. *Stay.*

Don't fly. That's not one of my commands, but it should be. Because my muscles twitch to try it. To jump like they're jumping. *Don't fly, Daisy.*

The Colonel cringes and smiles too tightly around all this chaos, but he's *here*, not gone, not in the cloudy white zone. It's making the rest of our pack very happy. Anna smiles at him, hands him the baby. "The tae kwon do studio was a good idea," she says. He nods. "Can you imagine trying to do this in our home?" she says. He shakes his head.

He hugs her with one arm. "It's perfect, *querida*. Look at those wild kids."

And Anna does, and she smiles, too. Today is a yellow day. She flits over to the food: cake and hot dogs that make my nose hairs tingle. Heaven on a tabletop. I watch her float between the chow and the curly ribbon presents and the humans here from other packs. She smiles and laughs and spreads yellow joy everywhere, as happy and free and swishy as a large park of wide-open grass.

But Anna is also a fence. She's gentle and joyful,

but she keeps her pack together. It's tough to do both. It's tough to be a wide-open joyful park and a safe-guarding protective fence. Anna does both. She's like a herd dog, that one. Impressive.

While the boys fly, Anna lights twelve sticks on fire and jabs them into the cake. My fur crinkles at this, and I pant a little. But no one else seems concerned about these little hot danger sticks of fire. So I command myself: *Sit, Daisy. Stay. Don't fly.* But I've got my eye on that fire.

All the humans start singing the same song:

> *"Feliz cumpleaños a ti*
> *feliz cumpleaños a ti*
> *feliz cumpleaños querido Micah*
> *feliz cumpleaños a ti!"*

Humans don't get a whole lot right. But when they make their voices come together in music, it's like cool, clear water.

Micah blows out the sticks of fire, which I appreciate, and I begrudgingly admit he's saved us all. People clap their hands for him, so they must agree.

Hot dogs. Cake. Ripping flying paper. Beeping flashing toys. Then, more boy flying.

Sit, Daisy. Stay. Don't fly.

Anna approaches me and Victor. She hands him a hot dog, which he gives to me, and OH MOUTH JOY DROOL. The Colonel laughs. "She doesn't even chew!"

Anna laughs, too, and it's like a flower garden in here, all color and honey. She slips her hand into his.

"I'm glad I'm here this year," he says.

"Me, too."

He shifts his weight off his walking stick. "That was the worst. Missing the birthdays. Holidays, all the soldiers were miserable, because everyone was missing Christmas or Thanksgiving together. But missing the birthdays? Solo misery."

Anna squeezes the Colonel's hand and his heart hums.

I don't understand why he's missed other birthdays, but solo misery? *That* I understand. And I understand that Anna was here while he was away. She made sure the birthdays still happened.

Victor laughs at Micah climbing up pegs on a wall. He drops my leash, his walking stick. "Stay, Miss Daisy."

Stay. Don't fly.

"I bet I can climb higher than you, *hijo*!" he shouts. He runs. He climbs, pulling his injured leg up the wall stiffly. His heart and Micah's heart sing together: cool, clear water.

Don't fly, Daisy. This is worth the Stay.

★ 7 ★

CHOOSE YOUR ROLE WISELY

Training to be a service dog is far away from life in a Dumpster. The whole next week, when Alex squeaks, "SIT, DAISY!" my tail is on the floor like lightning.

But training for two straight weeks now has made the Colonel soul-tired. Can no one else see his slumping shoulders, hear his slumping sighs? His moods are so twisty. Just a few days ago, he was scaling birthday party walls like a spider. Today after training, he drags both himself and me into the house, drops my leash.

"Wait here, Miss Daisy," Colonel Victor says in tired, cotton-puff words. He's taken a handful of rainbow pills again and he's mushy. He enters the bathroom and closes the door. I've learned that *wait here* means *stay*. Humans and their silly too-many words.

The bathroom is the only place I don't go with the Colonel. Alex pitched a hissing kitty fit when he heard that I don't go into the restroom with Colonel Victor. "What if you blank out in there?" he asked at our last session. "It's dangerous to go in there without Daisy."

"I don't know about you, Alex," Colonel Victor said, "but it's more dangerous for her to go *in* the bathroom with me." He winked, and that was that. The Colonel has a way of dealing with Alex that Alex isn't used to. I can tell by the constant shade of sour lime green that tinges the edges of Alex's voice when we're there.

I turn a half circle and get comfortable on the wood floor. It'll be a while, because Colonel Victor brought in a magazine with him.

Tick-tick-tick-SWISH.

My ears prick. My head cocks. Fish scales and falling trees.

Smaug rounds the corner. *Ah, young grasshopper*, he says to me. *It is you I've been seeking.*

Is that so? I ask and yawn. *You haven't been seeking juicy cockroach snacks?*

Smaug chortles oddly, like the flight of blinking fireflies. His long black tongue reaches up and licks his spiraling eye. *There are plenty of those to be had. No need to seek. Patience is all that is required for some rewards.*

I shudder. I've eaten bugs in my more desperate days. That's why desperation tastes crunchy.

Why were you looking for me? I ask. I'm intrigued by this animal. He's part of this pack, it appears, and yet he doesn't even pretend to be loyal to it. I can't decide if I admire that or if it endangers us.

Smaug's tail jerks with a crack. *You have not yet befriended Micah.* His lizardy toenails drum the floor. They are now painted goofy pink and blue. *I see you can sense need. And yet you seem to do so only when it is convenient for you. There is much more need here than you are servicing. If you truly wish to become a service dog, that is.*

A Smaug smog clouds my vision. My lips curl back and I taste oily annoyance. *You snooty lizard!* I growl. *You don't know who you're dealing with. You don't want to see me truly angry.*

Smaug rolls his eye. It's difficult to smell if it's disgust or if it's just how his wacky eyeballs move. *Anger is but a symptom, like a fever. Addressing a fever does nothing to heal the true hurt.*

Tick-tick-tick-SWISH. Smaug turns and begins to toddle away.

I can't help myself. I swipe at that irritating treecrack tail of his, and catch the tip of it under my paw. Smaug jerks about and drives two of his sharp claws up into the soft skin between my toenails.

YIPE! I snap my teeth at his tail, but the tip of it has broken free from his body. I'm left with a squirmy stump of tail under my paw. I shiver like chomping ice cubes. Smaug disappears around the corner, his tail an inch shorter.

Micah comes out of his room, just down the hall, one eyebrow cocked. He's holding a blue-and-orange ball, one too big and too springy to fit in my mouth. Silly of me to think Micah might want to play ball some time.

Micah sees me there. I cover Smaug's tail tip with my paw. It isn't what it looks like.

Or is it?

I am nervous about getting caught with a piece of Smaug under my paw. Nervousness tastes like a belly full of grass.

Micah squats next to me.

Poor humans. They must ache, having to stand on their two hind legs all day. It must hurt their backs. It certainly slows them down. I feel sorry for them and their uprightness.

"Miss Daisy?" Micah says. He doesn't touch me. He knows that's against the rules. Micah follows the rules. I have to admit I like that about him.

Yes?

"Listen." Micah clears his throat. His voice is a color that confuses me: iridescent translucent, like snail slime. Soft, but *what is it?* Is it sticky? Is it wet? He leans against the wall.

"I need to tell you: you don't get to be my dad's best friend." He glances at the bathroom door, picks at the wires coming from the ear covers that hang around his neck. Those infernal things. He calls them *headphones*, but *ear muzzles* is what they are.

"You don't get to do that," he continues, his voice squishy with rainbow slime. "That's my job, see. Best friend is taken. By me." He jabs his two thumbs at his chest. I am supremely jealous of human thumbs. "I am his best friend. Understand?"

Even if I wanted to bark a protest, I don't think I could, I'm so surprised. Micah stands, places the ear muzzles over his head, and bounces the ball, *thud, thud, thud*, all the way down the hall.

Several minutes later, we're walking down the street: Colonel Victor and Micah, dribbling his punchy, springy ball, and me, sporting my paper-crisp tan vest. It's the first time the Colonel has guided me out of our yard on feet. I'm proud to show off my humans, even if I'm still tail-chasing confused about what Micah said. How could he be the Colonel's best friend? He doesn't even have a leash or a vest!

"Wait till you see this one kid, Dad," Micah says. "He can dunk backward over his head and hang on the rim, and he's only fourteen."

"I bet you're pretty good, too, Micah."

Micah's face pulls to one side, showing his pride. "I'm not bad."

"How'd you find this park?" I can't see the Colonel's eyes behind his dark sunglasses, but I can tell by the shifting shadows on his face that his eyes are moving. He's scanning for danger.

Micah dribbles the ball between his legs as he walks. "It's at my new school."

"Yeah?" the Colonel's voice is tight like thirst. "You like it there?"

Micah shrugs. "Just like the eight other schools I've been to."

"Eight . . . ," the Colonel says. His voice flushes a light sunburn color. Apology. I don't know why.

"Yeah, so, this kid. The others say he'll play in the NBA for sure. . . ."

Tink. Tink-tink-tonk, tink.

The Colonel stiffens. Stops. He is an alert, ready fire hydrant. I stiffen and stop, too. "What was that?" he says.

Tink-tink-tink.

"I . . . didn't hear anything," Micah says, each word murkier than the last. He looks around.

My ears prick. I definitely heard something. It's a tiny, tinny sound, like a small cheap bell.

Tink-tonk. Tonk-tonk-tonk.

"There it is," the Colonel whispers. He lifts his chin at an object rolling across the road ahead.

Micah squints at it. "That? It's just an empty soda can, Dad."

The Colonel clamps his huge hand down on Micah's shoulder. "Don't move," he grinds out through gritted teeth.

"What?" Micah turns toward his dad.

"Micah!" The Colonel's words are knives. "Stay. Right. Here."

The Colonel's heart pounds like a jackhammer. He's sweating and his face is full of sharp edges; he's squinting blades. I know to watch for this. I've trained for two whole weeks, and I know. Plus, anyone with two eyes and working nose whiskers can tell he's seeing white. I tug backward. Colonel Victor needs to go home. I can follow my scent back home. I can lead him back.

"Daisy, *stop*," Micah says, turning his red glare down at me. But I continue tugging the Colonel away from the basketball court.

"We have to go, Dad," Micah says, his voice crunchy bugs. "We'll miss the game if we don't go now."

Colonel Victor's shoulders fall. "I can't, Micah. I . . ." He is full to the tip of his water bowl with giving up. "You go ahead, Micah. Go on to your game. You don't need me there."

I think of Smaug: *There is much more need here*

than you are servicing.

I wonder for a flicker if I'm making the right choice, leading the Colonel away. Breaking up our pack.

Yes. Yes, I am a service dog. I help the Colonel, not the rest of the pack.

The Colonel turns to follow me home.

Micah's fists are clenched. I know punch-ready fists when I see them, and I flinch. "I don't *need* you there, Dad. I *want* you there. There's a stupid difference, you know?"

Micah's eyes narrow like the tip of an icicle. He spits his words at me. "But *Daisy*. We don't *want* her at all. We *need* her. See the big, stupid difference?"

The Colonel's shadows cool. "You might be the first boy ever who doesn't want a dog."

Those words sting like too much sun and sand.

Micah spins and runs away, dribbling. He pounds the ball against the cold sidewalk so hard I'm almost surprised the concrete doesn't crack.

The Colonel sighs, an exhale plump with trashy defeat. "Let's go, Miss Daisy."

I lead Colonel Victor home, but I glance back one last time at Micah.

He should be careful which job he picks in this pack, Micah. If he wants to be the Colonel's best friend, he's not doing a very good job at it. And in my experience, when someone's not doing a good job in their pack, they'll be replaced.

★ 8 ★

DISOBEDIENCE TASTES LIKE DRY LEAVES

"LIGHT SWITCH, Daisy!" Alex squawks at me from across the dark, wide room. "LIGHT SWITCH." His words are pigeons. Pigeons are fat, nasty creatures whose wings should be stolen. Flying seems too big a gift for crummy pigeons.

We've just started our training for the day, and already Alex is unnerving me with his incessant squawking. We are at the end of our third week of training. I know this because of birdie Alex: "Three weeks down! Seven to go! Pick up the pace! BLOCK,

Daisy! CHECK, Daisy! WATCH, Daisy! SQUAWK!"

Today, Alex stands next to a silver metal plate on the wall. He points at it. Colonel Victor unhooks my leash and crosses the room, stands next to Alex. I know I have his approval to trot over there.

I do, and I nudge the knob with my nose. It's not pain-free, but *hey*! The lights come on! So *that's* how that works. Now I can make my own personal sunrise. Colonel Victor claps happy purple flowers, and I smile. Micah, who is here in the corner when he's not in the building called *school*, ignores my superpowers, as always.

"GOOD GIRL, DAISY!" Alex gives me a tasty bacon treat, then clicks a tiny piece of plastic that rests in the palm of his hand. *Click-CLICK!* It's the sound of bones breaking. It's the first time he's made this noise. I cock my head.

It's loud, this clicker, and it echoes through the space. Giant bones snapping all around us. I know the second I hear it that the Colonel doesn't like it. I feel his shade deepening.

Alex jogs across the room to the other light switch. The Colonel goes with him. "Again, Daisy. LIGHT SWITCH. Again!"

I look to Colonel Victor, but he seems okay other

than his shadows growing slightly gloomier. So I cross the room, too, and nudge the light switch down with my chin. The sun sets. Power!

"Good dog!" I get another bacon treat and another click: *Click-CLICK!* More broken bones. I flinch because I worry about Colonel Victor. Worry tastes green and sludgy, like algae on a pond.

The Colonel shifts. Even in the dark room I can see his face tinge darker. His heart races slightly.

He doesn't like the clicker.

Alex sprints back across the room. The Colonel walks behind him. "One more time, girl. LIGHT SWITCH."

No.

Alex taps the metal plate. "C'mon girl. LIGHT SWITCH."

Can't you see the Colonel hates it when you click that thing?

Alex looks at Colonel Victor. "Huh. I don't understand. She was doing great."

The Colonel gulps in breath. He's practically panting, and he's hot and thirsty and radiating rays of nervousness, like *his* belly is full of algae. "What's that you're using?"

"Treats," Alex says, jostling the bacon-filled

69

pouch attached to his belt.

Colonel Victor rolls his eyes, and I can smell his impatience from here. "Not that." He points at Alex's fist. "The clicker."

"Oh." Alex flashes his palm at the Colonel. A small blue piece of plastic is there. "Yeah. I figured it was time to start with it. We use the clicker in conjunction with the treats when the dogs do something good. Eventually, we just have to click to reward them."

I get rewarded with a stupid click? Thievery!

"She doesn't like it," Colonel Victor says. His voice is firm and solid, a brick.

Well, technically, I don't like it because YOU don't like it, Colonel. But true. Getting rewarded with a click stinks.

Alex smirks like the curve of an onion. "What? Dogs love these things." He clicks it again haphazardly— *Click-CLICK!* It's a thighbone shattering.

Colonel Victor cringes. I stand and push my ears back, because I will forcibly remove that thing from Alex's hand if I have to. I feel the hairs down my spine standing on edge. My anger tastes strong like skunk spray. I can have trouble controlling it. I blame the first humans I knew for that.

"Wow, I think you're right, Victor," Alex says. He pockets the clicker. I take a deep breath and sit. That was close. I wouldn't want to show Alex who's really the boss here, but I will if I have to.

"LIGHT SWITCH, Daisy!"

I cross the room and flip the switch, making the sun rise again. I have almighty powers over day and night. When kids dress up in bright colors and zoom around shouting words like *KAPOW!* they wear superhero capes. I should be wearing a cape over this vest.

Alex smiles. The Colonel smiles. Micah doesn't look up from his tiny screen. He is as unimpressed as a cat.

"Good girl, Daisy! Good dog!"

Yes. Well. We didn't do away with the bacon rewards, too, did we? Cough up the treats, meat man.

"Let's take Daisy to the park and see how she does," Alex says after I've shown him sixty thousand more times that I understand the command *LIGHT SWITCH.*

"Outside?" I don't even have to look at Colonel Victor to know what he thinks of that idea; I can hear the fluttering feathers in his voice. "I don't like parks."

Alex cracks his knuckles. He's trying to think of how to say something, based on the eggshell-thin blue color of this pause. "Victor," he says. "It's a low-stress environment. We'll start with the park and build up from there."

Colonel Victor isn't convinced. His face shadows stay stubbornly deep purple, the color of a bruise.

"You and Daisy here are partners," Alex says. "She's been working hard for you all morning. You can't expect a dog to work for you if you're not willing to do some of the work, too. You're a team. Fifty–fifty. That's the workload." These are the first words of Alex's that haven't made me want to upchuck.

"A team." Colonel Victor lowers his mirrored sunglasses. I prefer when I can see someone's eyes, because eyes talk louder than anything. He nods once. He understands teams. "Fifty–fifty. Let's go, Micah."

Micah huffs porcupine annoyance but joins us. We walk around the block to the park.

There are all sorts of glorious smells out here, and I breathe in deeply. Wet leaves and dandelion and rich soil and about twenty steps away, a chipmunk den. The breeze is swift and cold, and my fur dances in the wind. I feel sorry for humans, that they only have fur on their heads. There is nothing more delightful than tinkling fur.

There's an annoying talky squirrel to my left, about ten steps away, shouting, *Bring it, dog. You can't climb trees and you know it.* There are twelve gossiping birds to my right, flapping in a deliciously huge puddle. But I know based on the tension in my leash that Colonel Victor wants me to ignore them.

We do two laps around the small park, and the Colonel's heart is thumping. But it's a red-blood healthy thump, not a panicked one. He's doing very well with his training, and I'm quite proud of him.

"Maybe you should put Daisy on your left, let her lead," Alex suggests, an arrow pointing the way. "You might feel better putting her between you and anyone walking toward you."

"That doesn't help me with attacks from behind," Colonel Victor says, but he does it and shifts me to his left. Surprisingly, his face shade lightens. I have to acknowledge Alex did that.

We all relax when the Colonel relaxes. Particularly Micah. Micah's heart is practically singing at the moment, which surprises me because he's not removed the terrible ear muzzles.

"Let's see how Daisy does off leash, shall we?" Alex asks.

"Off leash?" The Colonel's voice darkens like spilled oil.

Alex smiles but doesn't show us his teeth. He reaches down and removes my vest (and the sudden nakedness makes me more than a little uncomfortable, to be honest). He unhooks my leash. "We need to make certain she'll return when we call her."

I'm free! Oh, glory, I'm free. For the first time since I was captured by that horrible Animal Control person, I am FREE. My muscles twitch like crickets. I could run wild. I could chase that horrid squirrel. I could tease the birds, take over that delicious puddle. But I'm unsure what to do, so I sit by the Colonel's feet and await my orders.

Alex hands Colonel Victor a stick.

Colonel Victor nods ever so slightly. He doesn't want me to go, but he's trying. Fifty–fifty. He throws the stick. "Go get it, girl!"

So I run after it. AH, THE GLORY OF RUNNING! Every part of me is alive. My teeth sink into the meat of the stick and my jaws delight in chomping, my mouth in slobbering. Sticks taste like chewy delicious wildness. I bring it back when the

74

Colonel hollers, "Come, Daisy!"

After three more throws, the Colonel is humming inside his skin, he's so nervous being outside without me on my leash. "Can we, uh, head back in now, Alex?"

"In just a moment," Alex says. His voice is pushy. "I want to make sure she understands COME."

Like I don't understand COME. *That's first-week stuff, Alex. I'm all the way up to BLOCK and CHECK and WATCH now. COME—don't be ridiculous.*

The Colonel sucks in a tight sharp breath and tosses the stick again.

I have to admit, I'm having so much fun being off my leash that I don't protest. Freedom is a fast waterfall.

"The needs of a dog are the same as the needs of a human," Alex is saying, but I'm not really listening to his butterfly words. The birds! They're chirping so beautifully, I could just gobble them up. They taste awful, though. Feathers taste like gloom.

"Safety. Security. Food. Shelter. Exercise," Alex natters on.

I bring the stick back. The Colonel throws it again. It feels so good to run! My paw pads squish in the mud, and I shiver with delight.

The Colonel's muscles are tight when I return with the stick the next time. "I think we should go now," he says.

Uh-oh. I've goofed off too long and the Colonel is lost-ball upset.

"If you're feeling anxious, maybe you should pet Daisy," Alex says. "Train yourself to pet her whenever you're feeling . . ." He leaves the sentence hanging there, and the silence is plump with embarrassment that he can't find the right word.

"Dangerous," the Colonel completes the thought like a hammer on a nail. Everyone's face shadows over at that, especially Micah's.

I need to cheer him up. And the last time I cheered him up was when I disobeyed Alex, dragging that laundry basket of toys. I learned that early. I should do something yellow silly like that again!

"Come, Daisy," Alex says. He pats his leg. "Come!"

But I have a better plan. I decide to chase the leaves that are skipping around in the wind, chomping each one between my jaws and grinding them to dust.

Ha-HA! Look at me! Ptooo! Ugh. So this is what disobedience tastes like: dry leaves.

76

"Daisy!" Alex shrieks. "What are you doing? Get back here!"

Not until the Colonel cheers up. Ha-HA! Gotcha, leaf! Ugh. Miserable dust.

Micah hops off a nearby bench. "I'll catch her!" His face is serious, his words a promise tight as knots.

Aha! Notice my antics have challenged the young one! Chase me, Micah!

"Micah, no! Don't chase her!" Alex shouts. "She'll think it's a game."

Come and get me, kid. Ha-HA! Close, but NOPE.

Micah leaps and misses me, landing THUD in the dirt. *I'll win, Micah. I will.*

"Daisy, COME!"

Not now, Alex. I've got leaves to chomp and a child to outrun. Ugh. This is exhausting. And tasteless.

"MISS DAISY. COME."

The voice booms down on me like a lid clanging on an empty metal garbage can. I tuck my tail and slink back to the person who shouted it: Colonel Victor.

Alex huffs blue disappointment and clips my leash back on. He doesn't bother with my vest. I notice suddenly how cold I feel without it. "Most inconsistent dog I've ever worked with," he mutters, his words pinpricks.

Inconsistent is a new word for me, but the way Alex says it, it tastes awful close to *useless*.

Micah frowns rain and dusts off his jeans.

Worst of all, the Colonel scowls, points the tip of his walking stick at me. I cower, because I know sticks. "Daisy. You know better."

I do. I know better. COME is first-week stuff.

We walk in silence back to our car.

He didn't call me *Miss*.

I don't understand why that didn't work this time.

This pack is *inconsistent*.

★ 9 ★

HUMANS ARE WEIRD

The stringy, gushy inside of pumpkins looks like something I've eaten too fast and then thrown up. Smells like it, too. I want to walk away from the smell, but the Colonel told me, *Sit, Daisy. Stay.* I remind myself: *Sit. Stay.* I'm not disobeying anymore.

I remember how much I want to be useful, after I failed at the park a few sunrises ago. I don't want to fail like that again. I'm still not whole-hog certain what I did wrong, but I know *inconsistent* is bad.

Micah and Anna and baby Analise and the Colonel squish their precious human hands right into the pumpkin mess, squealing and slopping and pulling out globs of muck. Then they jab knives into the pumpkin and cut out creepy, fleshy faces. They top off all these oddities by placing a fire stick inside the hollow pumpkin and putting it outside the front door.

Humans are weird.

Next, Anna billows a cloth over a table. On it, she stands up a piece of glass, and behind the glass is an old piece of paper with two smiling human faces on it. "My *abuelo* and *abuela*," she says to Micah and Analise. They nod. And another: "Tía Maria." More nods. And another: "And of course, your sweet *abuela* Luciana, your dad's mom." That one, Micah studies. He runs his finger over the paper, his shades soft glowy pink. He feels a connection to this smile on paper. Pink means *I miss you*.

I am still sitting, still staying. The Colonel never tells me otherwise, even when he leaves the room. *Sit, Daisy. Stay.* I practice my commands all the time now. I'm getting really good at being useful.

Next Anna places bright yellow-orange flowers in an arch over the smiles. The flowers look like small suns but smell musky, like a push. Like they pushed themselves right out of the soil by their smell alone. She hangs pops of colorful thin paper and places

more fire sticks around (humans and fire! So igno-
rant to the danger!). Then she lights a stick that smells
heavenly sweet, like the inside of trees. Small wisps of
smoke swirl off its tip, whispers from ghosts.

Finally, she places bread and fruit and little rainbow sugar candies shaped like skulls around the table.
She pours salt into a bowl and pops open a tin can of
something that fizzes and crackles in small bubbles
from the hole in the top. She hums while she does
this, and Micah and Analise help, and it's all very
sunshine warm and yellow.

"*Día de los Muertos.*" Anna sighs. "The Day of
the Dead. I love the altars, don't you? They're my
favorite. So colorful."

I wonder why the Colonel isn't here. Why he isn't
a part of the *I miss you*s. Micah shifts, like he's heard
me think that. "Where's Dad?"

Anna lays a soft hand on Micah's shoulder.
"Remembering those who have passed on can be difficult." Micah nods with the tiniest of head bobs, like
a whisker twitch. "Not everyone can see it as a cele-
bration, *mi amor.*"

She adjusts a picture here, a flower there, then
steps back.

"There!" she says, and dusts her hands. Analise

copies her, and the three of them giggle dandelions. "Go get dressed, Micah. It's almost time to go trick-or-treating."

Micah leaps from the room like a grasshopper. When he returns, he's wearing a suit that makes him look like walking bones. Anna puts Analise in clothes that look like a ladybug. Ladybugs are pretty, but they taste like dirt.

"Let's go, *hijo*!" The Colonel picks up my leash (which I've been dragging about, thank you very much). Micah leaps again, and his clothes make him look like a bone dance. "Walk, Miss Daisy!"

Walk.

Anna and Analise stay behind, holding a bowl of colorfully wrapped sugar things. "Have fun!" When we go outside, the sun is lowering, and long shadows are creeping up from below to take over the day. I don't like night. Nothing good happens at night.

Micah swings a plastic pumpkin around, and I cower a bit, because swinging things are sometimes aimed at dogs. "Which house should we hit first?"

I cower at *hit*, too, because those are sometimes aimed at dogs as well.

But the Colonel snaps my leash, and I know I'm to be brave and keep up. "The Millers?" He seems okay

82

tonight. I need to be okay, too.

We climb the steps of the house next door. They have a hollow pumpkin with fire inside, too, and out here in the growing dark, it is creepy.

They ring the doorbell. Inside, another dog barks. My shackles rise, and I feel a growl beginning in my belly. *Block*, I tell myself, even though the Colonel didn't. I move between him and the door.

The door squeaks open, and Micah shouts, "Trick or treat!" to the smiling man standing there.

"Micah!" the stranger says. The dog inside barks—*MY HOUSE! MINE! MINE!*—but she's penned up. I know because I can hear there's another door between us and her somewhere.

"And you're looking good, Victor," the man says. He drops a bar of poisonous chocolate in Micah's plastic pumpkin. Chocolate is evil; my belly never ached so bad as it did after I ate a tiny bit once in the Dumpster. I feel the growl getting stronger.

The Colonel flinches but smiles. "Thanks, Tom."

We leave.

The growl flattens.

The shadows grow.

We do it again, and again, and again. After six houses, I am panting, confused. The Colonel seems clenched a little tight, too. The hollow pumpkins throw confusing light everywhere, kids dart and squeal in the streets, and the scent of poisonous chocolate hangs above it all.

But Micah! He dances, he leaps, his heart sings. Those bones of his are happy. The Colonel sees this, too, and he is trying not to crack. So I want to honor him. He is here, and he is trying to be here, so I won't pull him aside.

But his teeth are grinding and his breathing is getting close to the edge.

The next house is dark. Too dark. But Micah insists. "C'mon, Dad. This is Jack's house. He said his parents love Halloween!" Micah runs up the driveway.

Wait! I yell, and pull the Colonel after him. Why is Micah breaking from the pack?

We catch up to him and approach the steps.

Something feels wicked. Off. I pant. Drool.

At the top of the steps—

"AHHHHAHAHAHAHAHA!" An electric-wire-and-light skeleton cackles and jumps from a coffin, eyes glaring red.

I leap backward.

And the Colonel *cracks*.

He punches the plastic electric skeleton, then yanks it and tosses it across the yard. "Take that, you—" and he says a word that makes Micah flinch.

It makes the neighbor who opens the door flinch, too. "What the . . . ?"

The three humans stand there, panting and looking at the broken skeleton lying twisted on the wet grass, wires spraying from his bones. The pause feels like a pinch.

We all wait. Watch. See what the Colonel does next.

I've messed up. I waited too long. I didn't listen to my instincts. I didn't *block* or *calm* or *watch* or do any of the commands for myself like I was supposed to.

But the Colonel laughs. At first it feels stiff: he forces his shoulders to shake, his lungs to gasp, his face to smile. But slowly, even in the dim light of the creepy hollow pumpkin, I can see his face shadows loosening, hear his heart switch from a hammer to a hum. He grabs the extra skin around my neck and gives it a little tug, like I'm his reminder of *here* and *now*.

"Looks like that skeleton won't be bothering you anymore, Jill," he says.

The woman laughs. "We've had that thing for years. Scares the daylights out of me at least twice a week when it's out. Good riddance."

Micah laughs, too.

I smile and loll my tongue.

The Colonel's training is improving.

★ 10 ★

A TOOL, NOT A DOG

I don't know the human equivalent of a place that is fireworks and tulip gardens and taco trucks and marching bands and slow high tennis balls and endless grass rolled into one, but that place for a dog is called the GROCERY STORE.

We are halfway through our training: five weeks done, five weeks to go. Alex is really tangled up about this. He's been chirping like a cricket about it all morning. Days . . . weeks . . . Alex uses words that fly by with wings instead of words that stick to you, like *TODAY* or *BUBBLEGUM*.

Now, we—Colonel Victor and Micah and Alex and me—step on a cool, rubbery pad. The doors to paradise slide open with magic, and it's almost like I can see rainbow sunlight bouncing off angel wings, it's so glorious. Glory tastes like fine Italian sausage. Smells like it, too. Right. Now.

The drool begins. I have to slurp every few seconds to prevent myself from looking the fool, because *oh my*. The hodgepodge of smells. Bacon and eggs and steak and bacon and ham and chicken and bacon and turkey and lobster and bacon. It is a wide-open blue sky of smells.

"Okay, Victor," Alex says. His voice of late has less of an onion tinge to it and more of a mint-leaf tinge. Still too green and overwhelming, but slightly more pleasant. "We're going to put all those commands we've been practicing with Daisy to work."

Colonel Victor's face pulls down. His heartbeat speeds slightly. But he nods. That's what bravery tastes like: saying yes when you want to say no.

We walk inside and, oh, the focus it takes when all the smells are massaging my nostrils! We grab a clangy metal cart with a wheel that shrieks like a demon, but the humans don't seem bothered by it.

Right away, a pink smiley person greets us.

"Hello! Welcome to Heavenly Groceries! No pets allowed, sir!"

"Block, Miss Daisy!" Colonel Victor shouts, a too-gruff warning bark. But I do: I move between the Colonel and the greeter and plant my booty on the cold white floor. The greeter's face shifts from smiley pink to uncomfortable brown. A moment of heavy embarrassment hangs over us. Micah grinds his teeth.

Alex giggles, a palmetto bug skittering across too-hot sand. "We're training Daisy here. She's a service dog. See her vest?"

I puff my chest because I am indeed sporting my vest.

"I don't know . . . ," the greeter says. He's no longer a greeter, though. He's a stopper. A sharp-cornered stop sign. "Is she certified?" He cranes his neck, looks around the store for someone else. This tells me there is someone of higher rank in his pack than he.

"Technically, there's no such thing as a universally recognized certification for service dogs," Alex says. His voice is harsh like shells. "But . . . no. Not yet. This is perfectly legal, I can assure you."

The Colonel is sweating now, and spit is beginning to pool in the corners of his mouth. I perk my ears back toward him to feel him better.

The stop-sign man droops a little, becomes less sharp. He steps aside. "C'mon into Heavenly Groceries, then."

It wasn't quite the trumpeting welcome into Heaven I thought I'd get, but oh! The blend of smells and colors. It's fur-tingling splendid.

I trot beside Colonel Victor, swimming through each individual smell: roast beef. Salami. Cheddar cheese. Apples (gag). As I'm splashing through each scent, I feel Colonel Victor's heart speed up. His eyes scan the building. I can tell he's searching for an escape route.

When we reach the end of the aisle, Colonel Victor shouts, "Check, Miss Daisy!" I follow the command like a driven spike: I trot out in front and check around the corner. A woman is there, staring at a tiny electric blue screen in her hand. I acknowledge her presence with a tail wag. I hear Colonel Victor suck in an uncertain breath before twisting around the corner.

Micah places potato chips, ground beef, and— OH, GLORY!—bacon in our cart.

"Watch, Miss Daisy!" the Colonel orders. He's comfortable giving orders, so even though he's clenched tight like a fist, I can tell he feels strong. He's still scanning the store, though. I follow his command: I cross to the Colonel's right side to see if anyone is behind us. The aisle is empty.

We proceed through the store like this: "Check!" "Watch!" "Block!" I am a ninja. I know ninjas because the Colonel and I go with Micah to a class called tae kwon do. It's where the birthday party was, and we go there lots of times while Micah trains. Just like me in my training. Micah is important in that class, so he wears a uniform and a red belt. He calls himself a ninja when he ties it on. At the class, the alpha dog there said, "Tae kwon do is for defense, not for picking a fight. If you can guard against attacks, it's all you need." That instructor smells smart. Fighting is awful: sharp teeth and too much blood. The ninjas in the class block kicks and punches and jabs. They defend themselves. And that's exactly what I'm doing now, for the Colonel. I am a ninja, like Micah.

"Great job, guys," Alex says. I can tell that compliment is split in half for two of us. "Let's go check out."

We push our bacon cart to the front. "Block, Miss Daisy," Colonel Victor says when we stop. I plant myself behind him in line.

The woman whose face is colored electric blue by her tiny screen approaches. She never removes her eyes from her screen. Her cart screams toward me like a dive-bombing mosquito. I brace myself for the blow in *three, two, one . . .*

Yipe!

The metal jolt hurts much more than I expected. A flash of a pile of puppies getting dumped into the back of a metal truck comes to mind, but I shake it off.

"Hey!" the Colonel shouts. His face smears purple. "Watch where you're going, lady."

She looks up, dumb as a squirrel. "Oh. I didn't see your pet there."

Micah's teeth grit. He is bracing himself. I know about bracing yourself. The Colonel works his jaw. "She's a service dog," Colonel Victor growls. "Not a pet."

Not a pet.

"Why are you getting so upset?" squirrel lady asks. Even her tiny pointy teeth remind me of a tree rodent. "You need to chill out about your dog."

"She is a *tool*, not a *dog*," the Colonel says. This statement: it's a good thing that stings a little, like too much sun. A tool is practical, handy, useful—all good things. But a tool is also metallic, flat. Unalive.

The Colonel continues: "And trust me, lady, you don't want to see me upset." His words are written on spittle flying through the air. I nudge him to try to calm his jackhammering heart. He digs in his pocket, slams some green slips of paper on the counter.

"Pay, Micah," he orders his son. Micah isn't a tool. He scowls at receiving a command like this. "I need to wait outside," the Colonel says.

The Colonel limps away, tugging me behind him. He leans more on his walking stick when he's angry like this. The magic doors slide, and we leave the mystical smells behind us. Outside smells blissful, sure, but it's no bacon.

"Victor, remember: pet Daisy," Alex suggests. He has followed us. He always follows us. The Colonel nods, pets me too gruffly. He bends over, hands on knees, and sucks in air. I lean against him. Slowly, slowly, the shadows on his face melt and a little sunshine replaces them.

Micah comes out, bag in hand. His ear muzzles are back on.

"You get everything?" the Colonel asks, taking the heavy bag from him.

Micah shakes his head and shouts (I guess because of the horrid ear covers), "No. You didn't give me enough money. No bacon."

No bacon. My tail droops. But then, what else should a tool expect?

★ 11 ★

THE TASTE OF DANGER

My sleep is filled with nightmares, of ripped flesh and monstrous trashy trucks with metal jaws and teeth on their hindquarters. I know my flanks are twitching, and I whine, but I can't shake out of this dream.

"GET DOWN, BUCK!"

The Colonel's fire truck shouting snaps me awake. I leap off my pillow, prick my ears and nostrils to find him.

The closet.

Colonel Victor crouches like a tiger in the corner,

hanging clothes camouflaging him. He clutches a huge, curved, red-alarm knife. His heart hammers and his eyes are wide and white. His face curls with the colors of deep wounds.

Anna stands in the doorway in a thin, worn nightgown, a ghost.

"Victor, honey," she whispers, voice trembling, disappearing. "Wake up. Come back to bed."

"DON'T BE STUPID, BUCK!" he yells daggers at her. "THE INSURGENTS ARE HERE! THEY'VE FOUND US!"

I sense Micah now, creeping in the darkness of the Colonel's bedroom. I curse Smaug for not doing a good job of keeping Micah safe in his room. Useless lizard.

A cold rumbling starts in my belly. This is very, very wrong.

The Colonel's eyes narrow tight like a strangle on his wife. He's dripping sweat. "Get. Down." His voice is barbed wire.

I push around Anna and ram my skull, *thud*, against Colonel Victor's arm, trying to bring him back to us. He shoves me aside. My hip slams purple bruises against the wall. I whine.

Anna sobs. Micah sobs, too. Somewhere deep in

the house the baby screams, toenails scratching across metal.

The Colonel spins the flashing knife in his sweaty hands. He crouches. He shifts his weight, preparing himself to tackle Anna, who he thinks is someone named Buck.

The taste of danger is thick on my tongue: meat with maggots.

The growling in my belly grows louder. I lick and nudge and push against him, but it's not working. If his face was filled with the colors of wounds before, it's now filled with darkest night. Holes. Demons.

How can I get him back?

"BUCK!" The Colonel leaps at his wife, knife flashing.

I dive between them. The Colonel wrestles with me. The knife slices the pad on my back left paw, a crackle of white lightning pain. I squeal.

That does it.

My teeth sink into Victor's hand. I don't put the full force of my jaws behind the bite; if I did that, I'd destroy his hand. I know how powerful my anger can be. No, I only clamp down enough to break the skin. His blood tastes like oily rain water, like puddles with rainbows of gasoline floating on top.

The Colonel's scream flares red, then simmers down to a boiling orange. He stops punching me and pulling my fur. His eyes focus on the beads of blood on his hand.

His breathing slows, his pupils get smaller. His heart drums a little slower.

"Miss Daisy?" he whispers hoarsely.

I sit between him and Anna.

I growl.

The Colonel moans, then heaves, like he's going to throw up. His stomach lurches three or four times. He slings his arms around my neck. He wails like howling wind into my muzzle.

Anna turns and drifts away, tears streaking rivers on her cheeks. She grabs her pillow and a blanket and floats from the bedroom. She's sleeping somewhere else tonight.

I hear Micah creep closer. He peeks around the corner into the closet. He didn't see any of this, and blue confusion colors his face. His confusion shifts into black anger, however, when he sees the bloody bite marks on his dad's hand. I growl, warning him not to get any closer. Based on how his shades flare red, this angers him further, but I don't care. Distance is safety. I'm up close. Micah shouldn't be. (Stupid Smaug!)

My sliced paw soaks blood into the carpet. The red stain grows bigger, darker, like afternoon grows into night. My heart beats in the throb of the cut.

"Miss Daisy," the Colonel whispers. His mouth is full of foamy saliva, his fur is a mess, and he's still dripping sweat. "You understand, don't you? The military—it's a pack. You protect your pack, always. You understand that, don't you? No one else does but you."

Micah lets out a small sob at that.

The Colonel snuffles and drools, a bulldog. "Thank you, Daisy. You're my pack."

I clench my jaw.

Micah clenches his jaw, too. He is a shard of ice.

It's odd. No one asked me if I wanted this job. No one asked me to be a part of this pack.

They never asked if I want to stay. They order me to stay: *Stay, Daisy!* But ask if I'd like to stay? No.

With my first human pack, my job was to fight. They said so, and they'd put me in a ring with other growling, starving dogs. But I couldn't do it. I hated fighting. So they called me useless and left me to have my pups in a Dumpster. I couldn't do that job. Maybe I can't do this job, either.

This *pack*, the Abeyta family? They don't have a fence.

Next time I go "do my business," I could just run away.

★ 12 ★

HURT IS CONTAGIOUS

Two sunrises later, the Colonel still hasn't moved from his bed. Which means no one has touched me or let me out to do my business. I'm lonely and full and my pack seems to have forgotten I exist. Loneliness tastes like water from the cold toilet bowl, which is exactly where I've been drinking.

And I'm scared I'll forget my commands. We haven't practiced with Alex in many days. I worry that Alex is out there squawking words like *time* and *test* and *fail*. I've dragged my leash around the house, quizzing myself on what I've learned: *Block! To move between the Colonel and the stranger. Eyes! To look into the Colonel's eyes. Stay!*

Do I want to stay?

And I'm confused. A pack is supposed to protect each other, not hurt each other. I'm part of this pack, aren't I?

This pack is as unpredictable as an ocean wave. Unpredictable pulls you in too far, until you choke and gag.

Let the Colonel sleep.

But that means I've been sneaking behind the couch to go. The couch is thick and curvy and covered in fake flowers and next to an always-open window. If I squeeze I can fit between it and the wall. The Abeyta family hasn't found my hidden bathroom yet. Which is surprising. Anna is very clean—she follows me around with a scary tall mop sometimes—so I worry about what she might do when she finds my restroom.

The whole bathroom thing is cocked-head confusing to me. The baby—Analise—they let crawl around with dung in her pants all the time. It's quite disgusting, actually. Especially considering how tidy Anna is in every other way. Tidiness is sky-blue respectable. Toting your dung along with you in plastic pants is certainly not.

I limp out from behind the couch. My paw pad feels better, but it's not been easy to keep it clean. I don't know why Anna and Micah didn't fix this cut. They're not supposed to touch me, of course, and they don't. I don't even think they noticed it that night. And *after* that night, they've been talking and moving pillow soft. They seem to have forgotten the night happened at all. How do humans do that? Forget so much so fast?

I've been licking my cut constantly. The skin is runny-egg raw and oozing. I hope I don't get a bothersome infection. I hope I don't get caught sneaking out from behind this couch. I hope I don't get replaced with a different dog.

I hope I do.

Anna is feeding Analise in a rocking chair near the kitchen. She's singing. Her voice sounds high and soft and warm, like mother's milk. It reminds me of my three pups, and the warmth and joy of feeding them. I shake my head to clear the memory.

Micah dribbles his basketball into the room— *punch, punch, punch.* He stops when he hears Anna's song. His face curves upward. He sings along with her:

Duérmete mi niña, duérmete mi amor
duérmete pedazo de mi corazón.

Esta niña linda que nació de noche
quiere que la lleven a pasear en coche.
Esta niña linda que nació de día
quiere que la lleven a la dulcería.
Duérmete mi niña, duérmete mi amor
duérmete pedazo de mi corazón.

I once saw this person who drew on the sidewalk with chalk. He'd take his thumb and smear the colors together, creating a new, smoother, deeper color. Anna and Micah singing together sound like that— soft, airy, fresh, light.

Anna finishes feeding the baby and adjusts her clothes. "Impromptu dance party!" she shouts. She flicks a button on a nearby radio and music blasts out like a car horn. Anna holds Analise, and those two plus Micah leap around and chirrup like a silly herd of grasshoppers. They bounce and smile and hiccup giggles. Their faces twinkle like stars. I can't help but smile and wag my tail, watching them. They have decided pillow time has passed.

Then I hear it: *tick-tick-tick-SWISH*. And smell it: fish scales.

Smaug, I call out before he rounds the corner.

It is I, he replies. He is careful to stay just out of

Anna's sight, the sneak. Sneakiness tastes like hot dogs stolen off a cart.

I squat, lowering myself to look directly into his creepy rolly eyes. *Where were you the other night when Micah needed you?*

The lizard's tail scratches across the floor—*crack!* The tip doesn't even look like it was injured, it just looks shorter. *I did not sense the need,* he says.

Seriously? I shake my head, then my whole body, because heavens, this lizard gets under my skin. Like a bloodthirsty tick. *The night of the screaming? The yelling? The crying? The blood?* My paw pinches at that last part. *How could you not sense that? Aren't you Micah's protector?*

The lizard twitches, licks his eyeball, peeks around the corner at Micah. *Canine,* he says. *Your gifts are not my gifts. Earlier I told you: I am a healer, not a protector. I can fix damage. But a healer is not needed if there is no damage to begin with. THAT part is your job.*

I feel like he's trying to trick me, like he's pretended to throw a stick when it's actually tucked behind his back. *You want me to do your job for you? Lazy lizard.*

Smaug smiles, showcasing black bug bits stuck in

his yellow teeth. *Ah, but it is what every true healer wants: to have no purpose at all.*

Thick boots pound down the hall, like fists on wood. Smaug sneaks around the corner, back into Micah's room.

Colonel Victor appears. His face shadows tell a lie. They tell the story of someone who hasn't slept in days, even though I know he's been in bed for many hours. I'm confused by him.

So are Anna and Micah. Their music stops like squeaking brakes on a car. The silence that follows is fog thick.

The Colonel grabs his pills, swallows a few. He sighs leaves on trees. He ruffles the fur on Micah's head, winks at Anna and the baby, and pounds back into his room.

Anna and Micah hug, and I can feel their yellow warmth from here. I understand something now. With Anna and Micah, being around Colonel Victor is like walking across a sewer grate: a cold metal balancing act. One wrong step and your paw slips and you get trapped. So you must walk carefully.

Micah opens the back door and leaves it standing wide. His eyes flick at me quick as cold rain. I can't tell if he's inviting me to use the bathroom outside, or if he's inviting me to run away. So I don't move. Micah lifts one shoulder, lets it fall. He pounds his basketball outside and is gone.

Anna picks up a rag and scrubs at a nonexistent spot on the wall. Analise toddles toward me. I brace myself for the fur pulling that will follow, but it's better than toilet-drinking loneliness.

Hurt is a funny thing in a pack. It's contagious, like a runny-egg infection. One person hurts, and the whole pack carries the burden.

★ 13 ★

A TOO-TIGHT PLACE
FOR THE SOUL

Several sunrises later, I'm lounging in a yellow daisy spot on the floor next to Colonel Victor's reclining chair. His face is falsely colored again with rainbow pills. He's watching loud and shiny traffic jam television. I alert him with whines and growling whenever dangerous animals show on the screen, because those animals need to understand that this is the Abeyta den, and they are not allowed. The Colonel chuckles at that, tiny tired huffs like sprays of smoke. He pats my head. Says, "Thank you, Miss

Daisy. What a good girl."

My paw has healed. We've started training again. I'm a useful tool. I am a good girl with one good ear.

Micah pops around the corner. "Look, Dad!" He thrusts his arm toward the Colonel. I stand, alert. The Colonel does not like surprises like thrusting things.

"I drew on a tattoo, Dad, like yours!" Micah twists his arm. There are bright, magical colors there. If you care enough about something to wear a picture of it on your skin, it must be a large part of your soul. Micah's soul swirl looks like the basketball he dribbles, with a net and a number, and a red tae kwon do belt knotted around it.

The Colonel's turtle eye blinks. His heartbeat kicks up a notch. I inch closer. Micah slides his gaze toward me, a snake slicing through water.

"Is that . . . Sharpie?" the Colonel says, voice sand dry.

Micah shows his teeth. It's happy human stuff, not dangerous. "Yeah. Tattoos are supposed to be permanent, right?"

"Tattoos are supposed to be painful," the Colonel says. His voice echoes; it's coming from a hollow place. He chuckles like rocks crunching under tires. "Don't let your mother see that."

Micah shows more teeth. "You like it?"

The Colonel clears his throat. Shifts in his chair. His face pulls down. But he makes his voice the color of lemon-yellow pie: "Yeah," he says. "Looks good, son."

He's lying. Lies are when your shadows and your heartbeat don't match the shade of your words. Humans do this all the time. It's so confusing. Why lie? Isn't the truth always best? Isn't the truth the most heroic? The most useful?

Micah bounces on his toes like the ball he always dribbles. "Yeah? Cool." He spins like wind.

"Son?" Colonel Victor says, his voice chalky. Micah stops. Looks back. Colonel Victor is fighting to calm himself, like telling yourself *don't look down* when you are high up and teetering. I step between the two of them. The Colonel doesn't notice. Micah does.

The Colonel rakes the next words from the bottom of his soul: "Tattoos are for warriors."

Micah's face might split in two, his teeth show so much. "Warriors. Yeah!" He bounds from the room, a skippy, nimble frog.

The Colonel swallows. I can hear how knotted his throat is. He lays a hand on my back. I can feel how taut his muscles are.

He rubs the soul swirl tattoo on his own arm: a kingly buck, antlers so big they stretch up and over the Colonel's shoulder.

"I'm sorry, Buck," he mumbles, his voice sticky like peanut butter. "I'm sorry, Buck. I'm sorry, Buck. I'm sorry, I'm sorry, I'm sorry, Buck."

He's not crying. He's stuck in a too-tight place for his soul. He's rubbing his skin raw like sand.

"I'm sorry, Buck. I'm sorry."

I understand this. Buck was part of Colonel Victor's pack, and now he's not.

Buck is gone.

I understand this because I've lost part of my pack before, too.

My soul tattoo is my torn ear.

★ 14 ★

HUMANS ARE DAFFY

It's cold-to-the-soul raining. But when you're a tool and not a pet, you stand under a tiny portable room called an *umbrella*. It's a terrifying piece of squeaky colorful plastic. The raindrops ping against it like rocks. The wet air but not-wet me is puzzling. My whiskers twitch at the noise of the rain on the plastic. The Colonel doesn't care for the sound, either, based on his drumming heartbeat. But he'd apparently rather endure the bone-rattling patter than get wet.

Humans are daffy.

"But I have a car," Colonel Victor says to Alex.

Today Alex is mowed grass—a fresher, lighter green but still sticky and itchy and sneezy.

Alex nods under his umbrella. A dozen tiny rivers snake off the roof of his plastic room and splash down on my head, my paws. I shiver.

"Like I said before, we're taking the city bus today for training," Alex says, his voice an impatient ticking clock. "Nothing will challenge Daisy as much as the bus. It's only two weeks until her test. We have to challenge her every way we know how."

Micah doesn't carry an umbrella. He has a hood on his jacket drawn tight around his berry cheeks. He splashes—*kaPOOSH*—into puddles like a pigeon. Water radiates from him like glinting silver pinwheels. He's grinning and rather enjoying himself. It looks quite pleasurable, honestly. It would be nice to have fun in a puddle again.

Fun. How frivolous of me! I'm no more focused than a hamster. I concentrate on what the Colonel is saying. Need is heavier than fun. My need is to be a tool. Tools do not splash in puddles.

"I haven't been on a bus since . . ." Colonel Victor stops his words like he's been tripped. His jaw clamps alligator tight. He doesn't finish his sentence. Unfinished sentences feel like lingering ghosts. I get the feeling his last bus ride has something to do with his last pack.

The bus hisses to stop in front of us. It sends a wall of water over me and Colonel Victor's feet. The Colonel spits a tack-sharp word. I shake-shake-shake and Alex and Micah glare at me.

The bus doors scream open. Alex and Micah duck inside the silver tube. The Colonel tugs the leash, instructing me to get on. The steps are steep and slick and rubbery, like mossy rocks at the pier. I slipped on those once, looking for food. My paw hurt for a long time after that.

The woman behind the wheel pig-grunts. "No dogs on the bus."

Colonel Victor looks to Alex, asking *him* to explain, which surprises me. Alex arches an eyebrow at the Colonel, telling him *this is all you*, which surprises me more.

Colonel Victor swallows. "It's a service dog."

The driver's pig snout twitches. "She ain't wearing a harness. She doesn't get on unless she's wearing a harness."

The man in the front row of the bus looks at his watch and huffs snooty cat impatience.

"Harnesses are for seeing-eye dogs," Colonel Victor

says, his voice getting pointier and darker on the edges. "She's a different kind of service dog."

"Yeah?" The pig woman snuffs. She'd make good bacon. My hackles twitch at her. I start panting because the last thing I need is to get angry here, now. "Why do you need a dog?" she says. "What's wrong with you?"

The other passengers on the bus are seat-shifting uncomfortable now, a park full of pigeons fluttering over thrown seed. Micah grits his teeth, places his ear muzzles over his ears.

The Colonel's heart rate is thrumming. I can hear the words he's trying to get loose from his desert-dry throat.

The seconds last for minutes.

"This dog," the Colonel says at last, his words like daggers, "keeps me from killing you."

We got kicked off that bus.

Like a stubborn flea itch, Alex insists we catch the next one. The new driver never even turns his mirrored sunglasses our way. I wonder if he can see at all; his body angles never change, not once, while we climb aboard. If he can't see, I suppose we'll be just fine with this bus driver, then.

And oh, dogs in heaven, this bus stinks. Wet feet and unbathed human armpits and old cigarettes and brown and yellow and moldy green stains. It's torture, an assault. I'm unsure how these humans aren't keeled over vomiting in the aisle, but based on the smell, *someone* has. There's no place for me to lie down, not really, so I'm balled up at Colonel Victor's and Micah's feet. And when we start to move, it's nothing like riding in a car. It's a herky-jerky, chipmunk-twitch movement, all starts and stops. My stomach heaves, but I manage to choke everything back.

One woman with skunk-gray hair coos at me, her sounds fat and round and lazy like guinea pigs. Another guy with a wad of brown goop crammed in his cheek makes ghouly, teethless faces at me. I'm trying to stay focused on Colonel Victor and his cracking knuckles, his grinding jaw. But it's hard to focus when the kid in the seat in front of you is on her hands and knees poking you with a plastic doll.

If the test will be like this, I will have a thorny time with it. My stomach twists, and I start panting.

"Aw, so sweet," one lady who wears a nostril-burning amount of perfume says as she passes. "Can I pet your dog?"

"No," Colonel Victor says. His answer is a bullet.

116

The woman's eyebrows draw together at his warning shot.

Micah shifts, his face rearranging. "Daisy is a service dog," he says to the woman. His voice is floaty, a soft white cloud. The opposite of a bullet. "She's at work now. So no petting. Sorry."

The woman softens. It's amazing to watch how different her face looks after Micah says this, transforming from purple to yellow, a healing bruise. "Oh, I see. Well, I hope you let her off work soon. Poor girl needs the chance to be a dog, too."

The woman surfs away on a wave of perfume. The Colonel, ever so slightly, elbows Micah, the tiniest of thank-yous. Micah's face pulls into a half grin. He gives off the faintest scent of satisfaction.

And then, and then, Micah breaks a rule. He inches the toe of his wet sneaker forward and nudges me on the chin. An identical nudge to the one the Colonel gave him.

I am tail-chasing confused. Why would Micah thank me? I've done nothing for him. In fact, I admit: I go out of my way—like, lost-scent out of my way—to avoid him.

I am not Micah's tool.

★ 15 ★

UNTRUTHS TASTE LIKE TURKEY BACON

The backyard is little more than patchy green grass, rocks, shells, and sandy soil, but it's mine. There's a single palm tree that swishes and paints the sky, and trees like this one are why swishing sounds are always blue.

I'm sunning myself. The pleasure of sunning oneself should never be underestimated. My soul is green in the sun. It opens, and I am bigger.

I need to rest. We've been training over many moments lately. Alex says, "One week! One week to go!" His words feel like green-grass bellyaches, like pokes from a sharp stick. So I'm sunning myself after a long day of being useful.

Hheeeeeeessssshhhhh.

The sound I see is red and orange and yellow. A burst of flame. I open my nostrils to it and taste Smaug.

I follow the scent. He's around the side of the house and he's sunning himself, too, on a rock. His eyes are closed, and he's moving slowly, intentionally, like a poem of flower buds lining a tree branch.

Hheeeeeeessssshhhhh.

The sound he makes by dropping open his spiky bearded chin and waggling his tongue. It's the sound of hot, hissing, crackling fire.

A fire-breathing dragon.

Do you believe it? Smaug says, eyes still shut. I didn't know he knew I was here. *Do you believe the fire?*

I don't. I learned long ago the difference between fire in my soul and fire on my skin. *Don't be silly*, I say.

Smaug opens one roly-poly bug eye. *If you believe, it becomes.*

I huff. Not always. "Always" is every time. "Not always" is not.

Your belief is flimsy, Smaug says. He waves a claw

through the air like a breeze. *I am a fire-breathing dragon. What are you?*

I pull my neck backward, a turtle in retreat. *Pardon me?*

What are you? What do you choose to believe about yourself?

Beliefs are leaves: each different, each essential. Plump with green, full of hope and promise, each one supporting growth. Renewing.

If I could pick any leaf in a world of leaves, I'd pick the one that seems most important to my pack: the *tool* leaf. The *useful* one. The one that proves my first pack was wrong about me. But I don't tell Smaug this, because his point is I can become *anything*, anything at all, and that is simply absurd and untrue. Untruths taste like turkey bacon.

I think back to Micah and his flying-friend birthday party.

I want to fly, I say. That's not a turkey-bacon truth, that's 100 percent pure pork. Who doesn't envy birds? But me flying is as absurd as Smaug believing he's truly breathing fire.

Then jump, Smaug says. *You can't fly without jumping.*

I'm shaking my head so hard at this silly lizard,

my tags jangle. He jerks his whiskery chin at the big metal box that blows cool air inside the house.

He's daring me to jump off it. Dares taste like sardines, salty and boneless.

I clamber atop the metal thing, my toenails making horrible knifelike noises as they claw the ridges on the box.

The metal is hot under my paw pads. This box has been sunning itself, too.

Smaug spins his head so his eyes are almost where his chin should be. He is rubber-ball unpredictable. *Now the potential to fly exists. Jump.*

The box is taller than I thought it was, now that I'm up here. Why do our eyes sometimes lie to us? My knees tremble like butterflies.

Fly.

I close my eyes.

I jump.

My legs spiral through air, swimming.

And the second before I land, I feel it. I feel *flying.*

I smile, loll my tongue.

But I don't tell Smaug. Why give him such satisfaction?

Smaug's eyes are closed again, and he's hissing fire colors: *Hheeeeeeessssshhhh.*

I climb back onto the metal box. It's not easy, and it's sidewalk hot, but *flying*!

I jump again. This time I twist my hips and let my tongue flap. Flying!

I can't hold it back. *Did you see that?* I say, grinning. I'm grateful that Smaug is not an I-told-you-so kind of lizard. I-told-you-sos rank at the same level as tattletales.

Hheeeeeeessssshhhhh.

And again. I climb. I ready myself. I leap—

Hheeeeeeessssshhhhh.

"DAISY!"

Micah's voice hits me with a crack, like a ball hits a bat. I open my eyes. I don't fly. I crash. Onto Smaug.

Smaug curls, hisses. I can't blame him. Instinct is blood.

Micah marches to us, his feet furious. "Daisy! Bad girl, attacking Smaug! Bad, bad girl!"

And then he does it. He takes the basketball he's always holding and he throws it with all his might. It hits my jaw like a car bumper. Silver chrome pain shoots through my skull.

I duck my head, instinctively protecting my torn left ear, and tuck my tail. I am tangled-leash confused.

This is something my first pack would do. My heart knots with sadness.

Micah scoops up his ball, his lizard, and stomps inside, his feet tattletaling my mistake to the Colonel. "Dad!"

If you believe, it becomes.

I believe I need to stick to that tool leaf.

"Well, you shouldn't let that lizard wander around like that!" the Colonel snaps at Micah. He leans against me, taking the weight off his walking stick.

Yeah! I chime in.

Micah flinches. I swear, I think he hears me better than any of them.

"It's a bearded dragon, Dad. And he was here first."

The Colonel pinches the skin between his eyes, and the gesture gives off a high-pitched shriek, like escaping air. It only seems to bother me, though. I cock my head.

"Micah, honey," Anna says. She lays a hand on his shoulder. "You just have to keep him in his tank now, okay?"

Micah scowls at me like I smell of skunk. His feet twitch. I pull back.

"We know you love Smaug," Anna says. "But we need Daisy. Understand?"

Everyone is stone quiet except the Colonel's pinch. It's nerve-snapping shrill.

Micah scoots his chair back. He leaves. Anna sighs smoke. Victor pinches—*eeeeeeeeeeeeeeeeeeeee eeeeeeeeeeeee.*

I understand.

Smaug is love.

I am need.

But need is useful.

Right?

★ 16 ★

GARBAGE TRUCK WORDS

"Today's the big day, Daisy!" Alex squeaks at me, his words a pile of twitchy chipmunks. "Today you take your test. Are you ready to be a full service dog? Are you ready to earn your patches?" Alex shows me the important scraps of material and thumps me on the ribs. I feel his question echo through me.

For the last week, ever since my pack thought I was attacking Smaug, I've been grunted at, scowled at, and looked at with squinty suspicion. By Micah. The other two treat me as a thing. A tool. A need, not a want. That's what I wanted, right? Yes, it is what I want. Usefulness.

I am ready.

Alex turns to the Colonel, and his voice changes back to normal onion green. The way he changes his voice when he talks to me irritates me like a buzzy mosquito. "Let's go in."

In is not inside a building. *In* is through the gates of an amusement park on the beach. Humans are packed inside like rows of fish scales. It smells of funnel cakes and hot dogs and sweat and grime and joy and fear.

Colonel Victor's jaw stiffens. Shadows pull his face down, down. Sometimes I fear the shadows will never release their hold on him.

Micah bounces on his toes, points to a large ugly metal mountain. "Can we ride the Screamin' Demon while we're here, Dad?"

Colonel Victor shouts his answer, I'm guessing because he can hear little else above his hammering heart. "Sure. After Daisy passes her test. We'll . . . try."

Micah jogs in place, a ball itching for play. His face reflects the rainbow colors of the lights here. He is endless grass on the perfect summer day in this place. I can hear his heart singing.

Once inside, Alex approaches a fellow built like an apple tree: all shoulders, tiny feet. The sun glints off his furless head. I feel sorry for him and how cold he must be.

"Colonel," Alex shouts over the rainbow noise of the crowd to Colonel Victor. "This is Frank. He's doing the test today." Alex's voice isn't green when he says this. It's orange, like an arrow sign on a highway. Like it knows things I don't, pointing toward ways I don't know.

Colonel Victor's jaw is popping like firecrackers now. He nods once and hands my leash over to Frank.

Wait, WHAT? My own heart speeds. Nearby, a train screeches on the ugly metal mountain and humans shriek like bats. *Colonel Victor isn't walking me through the test?*

Frank's eyes barely twitch in my direction, and based on the way he holds the leash, Frank is about as kind as a gravel road. He has a silver hoop through his nose. I sit, because no one told me I'd be tested by a bull.

Frank jabs his meaty thumb between my ribs. "*Psssshhht!*" he snake-hisses. "Stand, Daisy."

I do, if for no other reason than to avoid getting

another jabby poke in my ribs.

Frank starts walking. His stride is much different from the Colonel's—his pace is faster and shorter, and I struggle to adjust. When I tug the leash, Frank *pssssshhhttt*s me and prods me in the ribs with his thick, rude thumb.

"We'll be back in ten minutes," Frank says. He doesn't turn to say it, so I can't be certain the Colonel has heard this news with his tiny, ineffective human ears. I worry he thinks I'm leaving him. I perk my ears backward to listen for his troubled heart, but I can't hear it walking away through all this noise.

Oh, the noise! It's a terrifying tangle of sound: screams and thundering music, metal-on-metal grinding, children crying, adults yelling, children laughing, adults laughing. When you mix all the colors together, you get muddy brown. It's hard to see and move through mud, but I want those patches. I want to make the Colonel proud. I want to be a useful tool.

"Block, Daisy," Frank whispers like dandelion fluff. His orders aren't commanding like the Colonel's. They are soft and too airy. I need to sort out his cold-breath words from the other six thousand words staining the air right now. By the time I do, Frank has *pssssshhhttt*ed me again. That thumb of his is thick, but I could snap it off with my powerful teeth.

When I adjust to the muddy noises, I realize how many smells have wings in this place. Hot dogs and gyros and ice cream and popcorn and cotton candy. My mouth is a puddle. And there, lying under all the smells, just on the other side of the giant terrifying metal wheel, is the ocean.

The ocean. It smells like salt and sand and coconut oil and vastness and beginnings. It smells like romps through waves and catching minnows for lunch. It smells like midnight snacks; an after-sunset beach is a fine place for a hungry dog to find the tossed contents of humans. It smells like leaping, joyful, leashless freedom.

"*Pssssshhhttt.*" Frank's foul finger reminds me that I don't have leashless freedom. "Watch, Daisy."

I do. I watch Frank's back. I'd rather eat slugs, but I want those patches.

There are so many dizzying distractions between the muddy sounds and the noisy colors and the fetching smells, but I can tell I'm doing well on this test. I can tell based on the tension in the leash. We turn, we stop, we climb, we reverse. I can practically feel the patches on my vest now.

"Check, Daisy," Frank wisps.

I trot around a light-spinning, music-spurting, kid-screaming thing. It has fake horses trotting up and down in a circle. I check. The only thing there is a fat, dumb squirrel eating a French fry out of a garbage can. The idiot rodent narrows his eyes on me but greedily keeps stuffing the fry into his furry face. *Go 'way*, he mutters through mush. A disgusting little spew flies from his mouth.

Manners. I cringe.

I turn to report my findings to Frank when I hear it: The red-alarm beeping of a truck backing up.

beepBeepBEEP

It's quiet at first, but grows louder, bigger, like all sirens do when they approach. Nearby sirens mean nearby hurt.

I freeze. I stiffen. I stop breathing.

There it is: the monster truck with teeth on its hind end.

It backs up to the garbage can. The squirrel screams and leaps away. Two huge claws emerge from the truck's sides. They grip the can and tip the heady garbage into its terrible foul mouth.

I remember:

I'm back living in the warm green Dumpster behind the ice cream parlor. My sweet, amazing litter of three smart, beautiful pups begs me not to leave. But I have to use the restroom, and no civil dog uses the restroom in her living quarters. I leave the Dumpster. *I leave the Dumpster.* When I return, a monster truck is dumping my babies into its foul mouth. I try to save them. I rip my ear. I hear their yelpy puppy screams.

They are forever good-bye.

Screams. The screams of Frank, the screams of silly humans zooming through space on metal mountains bring me back to the amusement park. I'm still frozen. Stiff. Unbreathing.

Frank scowls. "Fail."

It's a garbage truck word.

Colonel Victor's shoulders fall when Frank tells him. He whacks a metal light pole with his walking stick, and the *clang* sounds like heartbreak. He pulls at the fur on his head. He yells inky words at Alex, at Frank. Then he grabs my leash and yanks me—ouch!—out of the park.

My tail is tucked. I am not getting the patches. I am not a useful tool.

Micah's tail is tucked, too. His ear muzzles are on. He looks at the Screamin' Demon with saltwater eyes.

★ 17 ★

ITCHES THAT CAN'T BE REACHED

I have an itch I cannot reach.

I wriggle, bend in half, rake my toenails against my neck. But the itch is there, just under my collar. It pulses orange. My tags jangle.

The breezy tinkle of my tags stirs the Colonel. He tries to focus his foggy eyes on me.

It's been two sunrises since I failed the test. I've been using the restroom behind the couch again.

"C'mere, Daisy," Colonel Victor says, his words fuzzy like caterpillars.

I do.

He scratches me. He takes his delicious human fingernails and scratches all around my neck.

It feels like steak.

I close my eyes, but I can still feel Micah staring at me from across the den.

Disappointment tastes like bubbles. Bubbles are floating rainbow balls that look like candy but taste like soap.

"We're gonna try one more time, Miss Daisy," the Colonel says. His words are too soft. "One more chance to pass the test."

He scratches harder.

"I'll pay. Two more weeks. Yeah, I can pay that. We can afford two more weeks. We'll . . . find the money."

He keeps scratching.

It feels like filet mignon.

But the itch is still there.

I cannot reach it.

It's too deep inside.

★ 18 ★

FAILING DOESN'T MAKE YOU A FAILURE

"Potty, Daisy," Colonel Victor commands. I go.

"Inside, Daisy." I enter the training building.

"Get your leash, Daisy." I do.

"Get your vest, Daisy." I get.

"Sit, Daisy." I sit.

"Still, Daisy." I sit stiller.

"Go, Daisy." I walk.

"Heel, Daisy." I walk on the Colonel's left.

"Over, Daisy." I roll onto my back and show my belly.

"Right, Daisy." I turn to the right.

"Quick, Daisy." I speed my pace to the Colonel's.

"Shake, Daisy." I extend my paw.

"Snuggle, Daisy." I place my paws on Colonel Victor's shoulders.

"Wait, Daisy." I pause while the Colonel sits.

"Visit, Daisy." I place my head on the Colonel's lap.

"Down, Daisy." I lie on the icy floor.

"Settle, Daisy." I remain lying. That's a stupid one.

Alex huffs impatience. "She knows all the commands. I don't understand why she failed."

Colonel Victor shrugs. "It's disappointing this was a failure." That word makes me picture fire ants.

Micah shifts on his tailbone. His ear muzzles cover his ears, and he doesn't look up from his small plastic screen, but still he says, "Failing doesn't make you a failure. Failure is not trying at all."

His words are tiny, surprising belly rubs.

Alex makes a clicking sound with his mouth, like a cricket. "We'll keep trying. We'll just keep doing this, I guess." He doesn't sound whole-hog sure about that. He unclips my leash. "Free dog," he says.

Free dog. The command means I'm off duty. That I can relax. Play.

Free dog.

His words are tiny surprising bite marks.

Free?

I need to be useful. I need to practice more. I need to train.

I don't need to be free.

Do I?

★ 19 ★

PACK RULES

Some days are unusual, like tuna instead of beef. Today is a tuna day.

Today we train without Alex. Earlier, he said fluffy cotton ball words like "not sure how much more I can do for Daisy" and "need to focus on other clients." I agreed. But I didn't know it would get this weird.

I am standing in front of a roomful of Micahs in the building called school. Their eyes all poke me. My muscles twitch under my vest. The horrible white lights above buzz and wash out all the colors in this room. This place smells of socks and warm lunch meat and puberty.

". . . and that's what Miss Daisy here does for me," Colonel Victor says.

The Micahs all clap. It sounds like a herd of running bare feet.

"Thank you, Colonel Abeyta!" the alpha dog of this pack says. She is in charge of a roomful of Micahs. She has my sympathy. Sympathy feels like the sound of squeaky toys.

She places a hand on Micah's shoulder. My ears perk, because she's made contact with my pack.

"Micah," she says. Her voice is honey. "Would you like to walk your dad out of school?"

Micah's face is pink. "Sure!"

We walk down the cold, white floor. My toenails click, and the sound echoes off the metal cubbies lining the walls.

"I need to duck in here," Colonel Victor says. He shoulders open a door. It has an odd picture of a human on it.

This room is tinier, colder, echoier.

"Here," Colonel Victor says. He hands Micah my leash. "Hold Miss Daisy for a sec." The Colonel steps into a stall and swings the metal door shut.

What?

This is all so tuna.

Micah holds the leash loosely but firmly. He jiggles the weight of it in his hand. The leather and chains jangle. He tugs the leash. Not like tug-of-war. More like he's testing where the boundaries are. I understand testing boundaries.

"Daisy," he whispers. "Block."

I blink at him. Is he trying to guide me?

Do I follow? We are of equal rank, aren't we?

Before I can decide, the door to this cave crashes open. A small herd of boys gallops in.

These boys weren't in Micah's classroom earlier. I know this because I don't recognize any of their scents; they all smell new to me. One smells like the goop humans put in their hair, one smells like peanut butter, one smells like sweat.

The one in front stops like a deer when he sees me. But he smiles. Micah's heart skips. His chin lifts. He flexes his muscles. He's displaying his strength. He wants to be a part of this pack of boys.

"Hey, Abeyta. That your dog?" Hair Goop asks.

Micah's face ticks up. "Yeah."

No.

"You brought your dog to *school*?" the one who smells like sweat asks.

Micah shifts, shrugs. He is itchy uncomfortable.

"You're one of the military kids, right?" Hair Goop asks.

Micah sways from foot to foot, a small tree in a mighty wind. "I was one. Now I'm . . ."

My heart squeezes for him with squeaky-toy sympathy. He doesn't know how to define his current pack. Switching packs is as difficult as walking against ocean waves.

"Hey, doggy, doggy." Peanut Butter squats and quacks at me like a duck. Like Alex. He reaches toward me. I flinch.

I feel Micah tense through the leash. He steps in front of me, an orange safety cone. A block! "Uh . . . you're not supposed to pet her."

It's true: I'm wearing my vest, so no petting. Micah is trying to follow the rules. But Micah wants to be a part of this pack. I lean around him, offering to get petted anyway. I can step over this rule like a tiny crack in the sidewalk. Just this once. But Micah nudges me back.

The rules of the Abeyta pack mean more to him than the rules of this pack.

"Not supposed to?" Hair Goop asks. "Why?"

Micah swallows. His throat is dry. "She's my dad's service dog. She's a tool."

"A tool!" This pack of boys hoots and hollers like crows. They gasp and wheeze too much. Micah burns red fire beside me. The Colonel burns red fire in his stall. I can feel their heat.

One of them finally sucks in enough breath to puff, "A tool! Does your dad need to be fixed?"

They bang and clang out of the bathroom, small twisty tornadoes.

Colonel Victor bangs and clangs out of his stall. He splashes cold water on his face, dousing some of his fire. Micah tugs on his ears. I can tell he itches for his ear muzzles.

Colonel Victor takes the leash from Micah's slack hand. "Let's go, Miss Daisy. Micah, I . . ."

I can sense the words that are growing inside the Colonel: *I wish you didn't have to hear that. I do sometimes feel broken, but I'm getting better. I love you.* Those are the colors on his face. Those are the words stewing in his heart.

But instead he says, "Micah, I'll see you at home."

Humans are frustrating.

What a tuna day.

★ 20 ★

THE BANGY, BOUNCY SIDE
OF MESSY

Over the next several sunrises, we train every day without Alex. We go over and over and over the same commands. Every day is an echo. An echo isn't a real thing, it's a reflection of a thing. Each day feels more hollow and thin and colorless than the last.

"Can we get ice cream today, Dad?" Micah asks on this particular echo. The words are a fat pile of diggable dirt, full of promise.

The Colonel's face doesn't pull down when this new thing is mentioned. His heart doesn't pound with terror. He is getting stronger. "Hey, that sounds great, *hijo*."

So we take a different turn! Different! Variety tastes like candy red hots. This new sidewalk is lined with clumps of bright purple and blue gum and the grime feels like sandy salt and the whole street smells like bright yellow tennis ball hope.

And the ice cream parlor! It's chilly inside like tiny pinches of snow, but it smells of gummy bears and sweet cream. A poisonous chocolate undercurrent is there, too, but it's easy to ignore because the blue-bird lady behind the counter sings, "Would you like a scoop for your dog, too?" And the Colonel smiles—smiles for real, like a sunflower—and says, "Yes."

Yes!

We skip outside and find a spot in the warm white sun. Colonel Victor loops my leash around a metal chair leg and places my ice cream in front of me.

Bliss!

Ice cream is summer rain on asphalt: steamy relief of hot plus cold. Ice cream is forever happiness. I don't blame the ice cream parlor for my torn ear and my nightmares. Those things taste like garbage, not ice cream.

I lap up the sweet, sticky cream. I'm very aware of

the fact that I eat with my face. It's certainly messy, and messy can be smelly and embarrassing. But sometimes messy is glorious and squishy fun. Ice cream tilts into the bangy, bouncy side of messy.

We're sitting there, soaking up sunshine like blades of dewy grass, when a girl not much older than Micah jogs by. She's wearing the same type of ear muzzles that Micah wears. Her heart sounds heavy for how fast it's pounding, like it's trying to break free from something.

She stops. Pulls the headphones off her ears. Squeaky sounds shoot out of the ear muzzles like faraway scattering mice.

"Can I pet your dog?" she asks Colonel Victor. "I know he's a service dog . . ."

She.

". . . but he reminds me so much of the dog I had until my parents divorced." Tears well in her eyes.

She. But I forgive her this last one, because *divorced* sounds like the not-fun kind of messy.

The Colonel is in a squirrelly mood. He likes rules so much he's almost a muzzle, but today he says, "Sure."

I wriggle like a tadpole, I'm so happy for new petting hands. The girl's pink fingernails are like sunsets.

After several scratches, her face shadows fade, and her heart, while still heavy, thuds a little lighter.

Then she hugs me. Tight, like rock. Her heart against my heart, singing together. My heart brings hers back into harmony. It's solid and sure. Hugs are the keys that unlock our souls.

I'd almost forgotten. My first pack had many faults, but they could hug like fur.

She loosens, leans back, looks me in the eye. "Thank you," she says to my harmonizing heart. "I was having a really bad day."

My pleasure.

She lifts on her horrible, mousy ear muzzles, stands, and jogs away, trailing rainbows behind her.

The Colonel smiles sunbeams. Stands. "I'm going to get an ice cream for Anna and Analise. Watch Miss Daisy, Micah."

Micah stares at him like he's a stranger, then looks at me the same way. He leans down to me. I flinch because I can't read his face shadows.

"How do you do it?" he whispers to me. "How do you absorb all those bad feelings?"

He fiddles with the strings of his own ear muzzles. "I've tried, you know? I've tried to be the sponge. But I can't do it. I can't."

His words confuse me like wind. *You don't need to do that. That's my job in this pack.*

Micah's face softens. But he chews the inside of his cheek. "I guess I don't need to do that, do I? That's your job in this family."

★ 21 ★

SECOND CHANCES

All five of us in the Abeyta pack spend the day at the park. Only twice do I have to nudge Colonel Victor to calm his twitchy heart: once when a tasty Frisbee flew by, once when a kid cracked a ball against a bat. Two times is quite an improvement. The Colonel's training is coming along rather nicely.

We ride home in the glorious wind-blast, music-blast car. When the five of us topple toward the house, sun-tired and grass-smelling, the Colonel pauses at the threshold of the front door, a pointing retriever.

He extends an arm, holding his human pack

members back. "Light switch, Miss Daisy," he orders.

I step inside, across the monster shadows flying throughout the house, and flick the lights with my nose. *Click!* The monster shadows scatter.

"Sweep, Miss Daisy," Colonel Victor commands. He's still not allowing his other pack members inside. I know how important it is for him to determine that a place is safe before his pack enters. This is an important job. I am an important pack member for doing it.

So I sweep. I sniff around each corner of our den, making sure there is no danger. I do this every time we arrive home now. A two-minute sweep through the entire house, then I report back to the Colonel that all's clear.

Analise begins wailing, a noise that tastes like black pepper. The sound makes it difficult to smell clearly. But I sniff around this room and move into the next. Micah's room.

Fish scales.

Welcome, canine companion. Smaug sighs at me. He's not in his glass box like he's supposed to be; he's curled inside the cup of a baseball glove, chewing on the leather threads. *All is well in Micah's chambers. That I can assure you.*

I'll be the judge of that, I reply. I know I sound

whiny like a throbbing stubbed toe, but this is *my* job. I won't be replaced by some lazy, leather-chewing lizard. Plus, he never even tried to explain to Micah that I *wasn't* attacking him that day outside.

I sniff around Micah's room. A wad of gum stuck under his bed frame. Skunky socks on the floor. A rotten apple core that missed the trash can.

All clear, I proclaim. Two more rooms to go.

Pause, Smaug says. *Listen closer.*

I think at first he means here and now, in this dot in time and space. I cock my head and listen to my pack outside. Analise is really wailing now, and it sounds like a red-and-chrome fire truck. It's difficult to listen to because it confuses my smell. Anna coos, *shhh, shhh*, over and over. Micah pops a bubble and I can hear from his huffs that he's rolling his eyes. The Colonel's heart pounds and he's trying to catch his breath.

I need to finish my sweep, I say.

You need to do as I say, Smaug says. *Listen closer. This is for you, not for me.*

I start panting. *I don't really have time for this right—*

Listen closer to Micah, Smaug says through gooey yellow teeth. *You're missing the big clue.*

YOU listen! I growl at this pile of scales. *I'm tired of you giving me advice. Micah is NOT MY RESPONSIBILITY.*

"Miss Daisy!"

I twist. Over my shoulder, Colonel Victor fills the doorway into Micah's room. He's wheezing now, and foamy spittle is pooling at the corners of his mouth. His eyes are black stones. Shadows stain his face, and his heart roars. Micah, Anna, and Analise peek around him, leaves on a tree.

Oh no. I got sidetracked on my sweep, and I've scared the Colonel.

"What's taking you so long? Did you find . . . ?" The Colonel pauses, looks from me to Smaug. The smug Smaug never stops chewing leather, never tries to explain that my delay is his fault. He is making me look duck-silly again. His gummy yellow slurps make me ill.

"You got distracted by the bearded dragon?" the Colonel asks. He blinks, jabs a finger at me. "Daisy! You should know that scent by now! Smaug is part of our family! I've given you a second chance, Daisy, and you keep making silly mistakes! You shouldn't be afraid of something you know. YOU SHOULDN'T BE AFRAID OF YOUR FAMILY!"

Shame. It tastes bitter like acorns.

The Colonel bends in half, hands on knees, and sucks in air. "I gave you a second chance, Daisy. I believe in second chances."

I rush to his side, nudging him, leaning on him, licking his knuckles. *I'm sorry*, I say. *I'm sorry*.

He trembles, like twitching whiskers trying to figure out the world. Behind him, Micah is a knot of muscle and tears. He and Anna and Analise walk away. It's just me and the Colonel now.

"I don't think this is working," the Colonel says, standing bolt upright. "This second chance. It's not working."

His voice is quivery and unsure. His words smell like despair. Like roadkill.

And I know: I've made the biggest mistake yet.

If I've destroyed the Colonel's belief in second chances, then, well . . .

I've destroyed his belief in himself.

★ 22 ★

THREE WORDS THAT MAKE A WHOLE POEM

The beach smells yellow and tan and blue and green. It tastes like stardust and universes and beginnings. It feels like freedom and ease and power. And somehow, it makes you feel both large and small. One grain of sand. Many.

I sit on the beach under a rainbow-colored umbrella, next to Colonel Victor and Anna. Analise digs in the sand nearby. Micah squeals and leaps through water like a dolphin.

I love dolphins. They sing to the soul.

The sand beneath me feels warmly shifty and impermanent. It feels like doubt.

"Tomorrow's Monday," the Colonel says to Anna. "The shelter will be open. We'll go see about a new dog then."

A.

New.

Dog.

Three words with enough power to tear apart a heart.

A wave crashes onto shore like all of earth is behind it, pushing it. Micah squeals lightning bolts of joy.

I lie down. Pant. I have water, but I don't want water. I can't get comfortable.

I want permanence.

But I'm sitting on sand.

The sun moves across the sky like a snail. Micah crashes toward us, spraying silver behind him.

"The water is cold, but it's *awesome*," Micah pants.

Gosh, I'm weary.

Weariness is thin. Murky. Gray.

Anna starts packing up stuff. She looks at the crust of the peanut butter and jelly sandwich Micah left behind. She tosses it to me. I gobble it up. It's sandy.

Micah towels himself. I feel sorry for humans yet again, that they can't just give themselves a good shake to dry off.

Look at me. Feeling sorry for humans.

I have to stop that.

"So the shelter, then," the Colonel says. He stands. Dusts sand off his swim trunks. His eyes don't meet mine. Cowardice tastes like roadkill. "Tomorrow."

"Tomorrow?" Micah's voice is oddly squeaky and hairy and mouse-like. He shakes his head. "I don't understand. We've been training with Daisy—"

"*I've* been training with Daisy," the Colonel spits. Regret colors his face immediately. "It's just . . ." He sighs. I'm beginning to really dislike sighing. Sighs move like snakes.

"I don't think a dog like Daisy can do this job," the Colonel says.

I'm unsure what he means by that. *A dog like Daisy.* A dog with a torn ear? A dog with a patch over her eye? A dog that isn't a fighter? A dog that isn't useful?

But I know for certain: there have never been thornier words than those. I sigh snakes.

Micah's face scrunches to one side, which makes it difficult to read his shadows. His heart skips faster. He gulps air. "You're making a mistake, Dad."

He's standing up to the alpha dog. It takes bravery to do that. The sunset behind Micah colors him yellow and orange. He casts a tall shadow.

"You know there had to be some reason she failed that test the first time around," he says. "And you've been training with her since then. She's so close! It'd be crazy not to try the test again. Why not give her one more chance?"

One.

More.

Chance.

Three words that make a whole poem.

The Colonel cracks his knuckles. Grits his teeth. I'm fully prepared for him to slip out of sync, or for him to get spears in his eyes. Micah braces himself like a palm tree facing a storm.

But the Colonel nods. It's a small, simple thing that humans do, nodding. But a small, simple *yes* can be a very big thing.

"One more chance," Colonel Victor mutters. "Maybe." He turns to pack up a cooler. "We are close to the new test date. Okay."

Micah's grin tilts toward his mom. She shoots him a discreet thumbs-up.

Surprise tastes like cinnamon.

But here's the thing that Micah forgot: he forgot to convince *me*.

On the ride home, I sit in the back of the glorious car between Analise's seat and Micah with the ear muzzles. Colonel Victor and Anna discuss a new medicine the Colonel is taking, and they say windy words like *side effects* and *drowsy* and *diarrhea*.

Micah's face ticks up on that last one.

How does he hear with those things on his ears?

The swaying car makes me drowsy. I spin, lie down, curl up tight. When I wake, my head is somehow resting on Micah's leg. His hand is light on my neck. He smiles at me as I smack my drooling jaws awake.

Humans are full of cinnamon.

★ 23 ★

DISOBEDIENT DAISY

The sidewalk is sausage-sizzling hot under my paw pads. The traffic on the road next to us is full of green and orange and blue and red and yellow and silver noises and reminds me of Analise. Horns honk and sirens warn and engines rev and all of it together is too much flavor and it makes my nervous stomach churn.

We're headed to take the certification test again.

Nervousness tastes like pigeon feathers.

"I don't understand why I can't walk her through

the test," Colonel Victor says in chisel-sharp words. "She's my service dog."

"That's exactly why you can't administer the test," Alex says. His words today are flat and black like tire marks. "You're biased."

Not in a positive way, I chime in.

Micah scuffs his feet on the sidewalk next to me, and the noise makes me itchy because it sounds like fleabites. His ear muzzles cover his ears again, and for once, I'm jealous of them, because then I wouldn't have to suffer this clatter.

"It's ridiculous," the Colonel says. "Miss Daisy doesn't need to be certified."

He doesn't think I can pass this test. I might agree with him. Doubt tastes like heartworm medicine.

"She does if you want the VA to cover her bills," Alex says.

Alex, go play in that traffic.

"The VA is a pile of . . ." The Colonel's heart rushes. He leaves that sentence hanging there, but there are very few things that pile, and almost all of them stink.

The Colonel grits his teeth. I can tell by the twist of shadows on his face that his stomach is knotted just like mine.

Alex natters on about the test, using long-legged, spidery words like *proficient* and *competent* and *pliable*.

All of it, together, is too much. I'm feeling dizzy, tail-chasing dizzy, when I hear it:

BeepBeepBEEP.

It's a sneaky, snaky sound that creeps like black ink under all the other sounds.

BeepBeepBEEP.

It gets louder. The Colonel seems to sense it, too, because his heart explodes and his eyes glass over, full of milky ghosts.

BeepBeepBEEP.

We're approaching a crosswalk. Alex swings his arms around grandly, chattering. A stupid squirrel. He doesn't notice.

I dig in.

I sit on that scalding-hot sidewalk, roasting my rear end.

"Walk, Daisy!" Alex orders.

The leash yanks my neck, and I gag.

BeepBeepBEEP.

"Walk, Daisy!" Alex shouts at me. It sounds like he's underwater.

I disobey.

Alex's words from early in our training burn in my mind: *There's a difference between a smart dog and an obedient dog, and for this job, we need an obedient dog.*

"Walk, Daisy!"

I disobey.

The Colonel is shaking now, a full-body *no*.

Micah plants himself, too. Grabs his dad's arm. He's brave to touch his dad when the Colonel is out of sync.

BeepBeepBROOOOOOOOOWWWWWWW.

A truck roars past in reverse, cutting the corner too quickly. The wind it creates as it whooshes by us is full of sewer stink.

Alex's eyes widen. "That was . . ." His voice catches in his throat.

"Close." Micah says. He pulls his arm away from the Colonel like he's touched something boiling hot. Micah is shaking, and his eyes are wide, his breathing short and shallow.

I know those signs.

I can help.

I step forward, nudge Micah's knee with my cold nose. I rub the side of my head, my torn ear, on his leg. I lean on him, my ribs against his shin.

He lays his fingertips on my head. His heart slows, his breathing deepens.

He bends down. Looks me directly in the eye.

When humans look dogs directly in the eye, their souls soften.

Both souls.

"You heard that truck, didn't you?" he whispers.

Yes. I'm panting now. *And so did you.*

Smaug's voice is now in my mind: *Listen closer to Micah. You're missing the big clue.*

The ear muzzles.

Micah's ear muzzles don't make squeaky music noises like that jogger girl's did. His ear muzzles are always, always, completely quiet. And the Colonel and Anna and Alex and other tall humans talk about all sorts of things once he puts them over his ears.

Micah doesn't wear ear muzzles to listen to *other* things.

Micah wears ear muzzles to listen to *now.*

He doesn't turn music on. The others *think* he does, and then they talk about all sorts of tall human things. He's tricked them so he can know what's going on. The ear muzzles are useful.

I am so confused. So dizzy. My throat hurts from the yanked leash and my butt hurts from the hot sidewalk and my head hurts from these windy humans.

My stomach lurches. Once, twice, three times.

I vomit.

I fail the test.

Again.

The Colonel is so tired he doesn't even scowl at me.

Alex is so upset he doesn't even smirk at me.

Micah is so suspicious he doesn't take his eyes off me.

Micah knows.

He knows I failed the test on purpose.

There are no scent maps with this pack. I don't understand them. And if I don't understand, how can I help? How can I be a useful part of it?

I try my hardest to be useful, and it's wrong. I make a mistake, and it's right. Lizards and knives and ear-muzzle lies confuse me. And any good choice I make outside the test doesn't count. Humans and numbers and tests! So little faith in instinct! How do they possibly survive thinking so often with their brains and so rarely with their hearts?

Colonel Victor and I are like two pups from the same litter: we've both lost dear members of our pack.

We're both fighters who don't want to fight anymore. And now I've even destroyed his belief in second chances. Destroying things is worse than uselessness. That makes me even worse than before.

There's a difference between a smart dog and an obedient dog, and for this job, we need an obedient dog.

I knew I had to fail the test when I disobeyed Alex at the crosswalk. He wants a mushy, pliable dog, not one that disobeys when he says *walk*.

I am not an obedient dog.

So I failed the test on purpose.

Micah stood up for me, fought for one more chance for me, but I can't do it. I threw his chance away like garbage.

★ 24 ★

RAINY DAYS

Rain confuses a dog. Cold water falling from gray skies coats all the colors with a film of silvery flash. Rain smears all the scents and washes them underground. There are no more scent maps, after the rain; the past is carried away, and finding your home after a rainstorm is difficult.

That's why lost feels like rain.

This pack, the Abeyta pack, makes me feel rainy.

I'm not useful here.

I'm not useful at all.

If I'd been useful to my first pack of humans, if I'd

fought other dogs like they wanted me to, my pups would be okay today. They'd be fighters, which would break my heart, but they'd still be with me.

Now the Abeyta pack will take me back to the shelter. I'll have another fourteen sunrises before I head through the Bad Side door. Unless someone else finds my use.

I can't blame them. It's dangerous for a pack to keep a member who has no use.

Today is a rainy day.

★ 25 ★

THE GOOD SIDE BELL,
PART TWO

This car ride is not glorious. It is stuffy and wind-less and full of the sound of tires moaning across roads.

We—the Colonel and Alex and Micah and me—pull into the parking lot of the shelter. I knew we'd come here, but I didn't fully think this through when I failed the test. The toy lightning cages. The cardboard dry food. The heavy smell of dog fear.

My leash jangles like a mourning bell.

My tail tucks, my head hangs as we approach the door.

Until . . .

That scent!

My head snaps up. I flare my nostrils and suck in the smells, trying to separate the taste of each.

It is! It *has* to be!

I start yanking the leash, my toenails skidding and scratching the pavement like tiny, galloping music notes. *Let's go! We have to get in there!*

"Whoa!" the Colonel says. "Easy there, Miss Daisy!"

The bell over the Good Side door dings green.

Janie looks up from her always desk. "Oh! Well, hello again."

But I'm pulling and jerking and tugging and skidding and whining and crying because—

KATIMA! I yell. I heave toward a row of cages, wrenching the Colonel behind me. She's in the middle one, too high for me to see.

I hear her stand, tiny flecks of lightning sparking off her cage like fireworks. She's penned up, but she's HERE. SHE'S HERE!

Is it you? Katima cries. *Is it really you?*

We're both whining and crying and pawing and scratching and OH! KATIMA'S HERE!

"Do these two know each other?" Micah asks. He looks at Janie.

She blinks like a possum. "It looks that way."

The Colonel's heart races. "Can you get the other dog down, please?"

Janie unlocks the door with a tiny *click* that sounds like a whole song. Before she can even reach into the cage, Katima jumps down to me.

I pull the leash out of the Colonel's hand. Katima and I wriggle and writhe and sniff and whine like a pile of pigs. I get us tangled together with the leash and we laugh and lick and cry.

Micah laughs. The Colonel laughs. Even Alex, who I'd forgotten exists on this day, laughs.

"Looks like they're old buddies," the Colonel says. By the way he says *buddies*, I know it's a word full of music to him. It's a word with weight and worth.

But we're more than buddies.

We're family. I sigh.

Mama, Katima says, licking my face. *Mama.*

★ 26 ★

RAIN SPUN INTO SUNSHINE

"She showed up here," Janie was saying in her meek voice. Before, I thought Janie's voice useless, simply because it wasn't bold. But useful isn't always bold. That was a mistake, to think that. Mistakes taste humble like dry dog food. "We don't normally get dogs who wander right up on us, but this one sure did."

Katima nods. *I did. I followed your scent all the way here, Mama.*

I lick her face. It tastes like sweet candy sprinkle love. *Smart girl.*

Alex stoops, looks Katima in the eye.

He's harmless, I tell her. *A dullard, but harmless.*

She sits tall on her rump, anxious to make a good impression. That's my girl.

"Hmmm," Alex says. He sneaks a hand forward, turns Katima's jaw back and forth. "This is one good-looking dog."

Like mother, like daughter, I say, and Katima and I both laugh with our tails.

"She's healthy and smart," he adds.

You are as right as a ball bounce, Onion Alex, I think to myself. *I love you and your poop-scooping and your caramel squeals and your kitty litter protests because you see beauty here.*

Micah's heart zooms. He looks to his dad. "What do you think?"

Colonel Victor grunts into a squat. He looks deep into Katima's eyes, then to me.

"Is this the one, Miss Daisy? Is this my new service dog?"

I fully realize what I'm doing: I'm sacrificing my position as Colonel Victor's tool for Katima. I will go into the cage and she will come out. She will become his service dog. I will become the useless dog. He wants a different dog, not another dog. It is the right choice. I would do it again and again and again.

171

I bark. *Yes, sir!*

If I could salute, I would.

The Colonel groans back to standing. "She's the one."

Micah clears his dry throat. He steps forward, and I recognize his bravery stance. It reminds me of a flagpole, strong and straight. "But we're keeping them both, right? I mean, look at them! We can't separate them now!"

His voice teeters on the edge of teary. Saltwater waves beneath his strength. And then he does it. He squats and hugs me, tight like fur. His heartbeat and mine, singing the same song.

I hold my breath like a windless day.

The Colonel pauses. Pauses feel like stopped time.

Colonel Victor eyes Micah, hugging me. He cocks his head. And for maybe the first time, he *hears*. He hears the heart song. He smiles.

"Looks like we're adding another dog to our pack."

I am so yellow-sunshine full of joy, I feel I might burst. I plop my booty right down on the large gray welcome mat and give myself a long, satisfying butt scooch. My pack—plus one!—laughs rainbows. Full, glorious, rain-spun-into-sunshine rainbows.

172

★ 27 ★

THAT'S MY JOB

*W*hen they say, *"Block," that means . . . ?*
I ask.

Stand between the Colonel and the stranger,
Katima answers. The Abeyta pack now calls Katima
"Rosie," but I don't want to give up the name Katima.
It means "powerful daughter."

And when you hear the command "Heel," that
means . . . ?

Walk on the Colonel's left.

Good. Now—

Mama?

Yes, Katima?

Don't worry. I got this.

I laugh with my tail. *I know you do. You're the right dog for this job.* I give her a quick lap with my tongue.

I watch her trot off, wearing the vest. Her head is held high like a police horse. She will earn those patches. She's worked for weeks now and she's a useful tool to Colonel Victor.

He's improved under her training, too. His heart is steady and his shadows less fierce. He has more rebuilding to do, but Katima's the right tool for the job.

We are unsure of where Katima's two brothers ended up. A swirl of pain and hope fills me when I think of them, like a sky both blue and cloudy. Maybe they can find us someday, too. I've learned good-byes can be unfinished.

"Daisy?" Micah shouts sunbeams out the back door. "Wanna go to the park?"

I bark. I wag.

Micah laughs dandelions.

"Car, Daisy!"

I dash around the side of the house, headed for the glorious car. But first—

Fish scales.

Smaug is there, sunning himself on a rock. *Ah, greetings, pet.*

Greetings, pet yourself, I sniff. *How did you get out of your tank?*

Yes, but my job here as pet is done, Smaug says, ignoring my question. *Retirement is in my future. My services as healer are no longer needed.*

Smaug looks tired like trees in winter.

What do you mean? I ask.

His eyes spin halfheartedly. *Did you find your usefulness?*

I smile. Pant. *I did. I think I'm pretty useful as a pet.*

Smaug nods, and his lizard whiskers swish blue. *I would agree. Sometimes we're not the tool we think we are. That is acceptable. We're all useful somewhere.* He coughs a little, and his wobbly chin wiggles like juicy fat on meat.

Are you okay? I ask.

I am more than okay, Smaug answers. He walks away, dragging his tail through the sand, *swooshswooshSWISH. I have healed. I am complete.*

I nod. *Thank you for healing Micah*, I shout after him.

Micah. Yes. Him, too, Smaug says with a chuckle. He snaps his once-broken tail around the rock and disappears.

I have the taste in my mouth that I'll never see him again.

Fish scales smell like astonishment.

At the park, Micah unclips my leash.

Thank you, I say. And he must hear me, he *must*, because he hugs my neck and his soft cheek is on my fur and he smells like clean grass.

"Thank you," he echoes, a whisper like a kiss. He squeezes me, and my heart squeezes him back.

Micah throws the fuzzy ball for me and I catch it and bring it to him.

Analise tugs my skin and squawks like a baby bird.

Anna feeds me a happy purple popsicle.

When we met, Micah and I both felt fireflies of hope. Those fireflies have turned into fireworks. Fireworks feel like love.

I chase leaves and chomp them into dust—*Pitoo!*
Pitoo! Ugh!

Usefulness tastes like leaf dust.

Which, to be honest, tastes dreadful. But it's
worth it, because it makes my pack laugh happy yellow sunshine.

And that's my job.

★ THE END ★

AUTHOR'S NOTE

Dogs fascinate me, and especially service dogs. Service dogs help humans in so many ways: they help sight-impaired persons navigate the world. They warn children and adults with epilepsy when a seizure is impending. They can assist those of us with physical challenges by doing such chores as retrieving shoes and turning on lights. And yes, they can provide emotional assistance to those with anxiety challenges, like veterans with post-traumatic stress disorder (PTSD).

PTSD is a very real battle for many Americans, and particularly for military veterans. PTSD causes anxiety and horrific flashbacks in those who have witnessed or survived a traumatic event. According to the National Center for PTSD, run by the U.S.

Department of Veterans Affairs (www.ptsd.va.gov), PTSD affects the family and relationships of those suffering the disorder. Those with PTSD have nightmares and experience anxiety attacks, which can lead them to avoid social situations. PTSD is often described as being constantly on guard and anticipating the worst.

I'm grateful to the brave men and women who share their stories of battling PTSD. It can be a struggle for these men and woman to experience daily life without extremely high degrees of panic and anxiety, and yet they courageously share their struggles, with the hope that sharing equals empathy and understanding. PTSD and other anxiety disorders are an epidemic among military personnel; it is estimated that twenty-two veterans take their own life every day.

Service dogs help prevent that. These dogs are highly trained, and they are effective at calming and protecting their handlers when the need arises. They help reduce depression, ward off panic attacks, and assist their handlers in the event of an injury. In 2009, Senator Al Franken of Minnesota introduced legislation to help provide funding for service dogs for military personnel. Since then, an estimated 220 service dogs have been studied to see the impact on military families. However, because it is difficult to know exactly *how* a dog helps those suffering with anxiety disorders, it can still be hard for a veteran with PTSD to find funding for a service dog. Funding for service dogs is often allocated to veterans who have physical injuries first.

I've tried to accurately depict the training these dogs receive; any errors within the story are mine. I am indebted to Katie Young of Southeastern Guide Dogs for enduring hours of my questions. Katie specializes in training dogs who assist people battling PTSD.

If you'd like more information or would like to sponsor a service dog, there are many resources available online. Check out the following organizations:

- Southeastern Guide Dogs, www.guidedogs.org

- Paws for Veterans, www.pawsforveterans.com

- Warrior Canine Connection,

www.warriorcanineconnection.org

An excellent book about service dogs is *Until Tuesday* by Luis Carlos Montalván. Montalván was a captain in the United States Army, and his story about his golden retriever service dog, Tuesday, is both heartwarming and eye-opening.

It is true that the handler can be the only person

who pets, feeds, and interacts with a service dog for the first thirty days of the dog living with a new family. It often does cause jealousy and pain for the other family members, who can struggle to understand why a dog provides such special support.

Military families—the *whole* family, not just the person serving—give our country their all. I am personally grateful to the Buttram family, the Durband family, and the Trew family for the many sacrifices they've made over dozens of years to ensure our collective safety and freedom. Thank you, friends!

And finally, I am a dog owner and lover, and my family and I often narrate what our two silly dogs— Lucky and Cookie—are thinking as they lope and leap and love their way through the world. In this story, Miss Daisy sees a rainbow of colors, and while it's likely that dogs aren't fully color-blind as is commonly believed, they most likely have a mild red-green color confusion. It is also believed that dogs experience multiple senses simultaneously, like a human with synesthesia might. Knowing these facts truly makes me wonder how a dog navigates the world, and the voice of Miss Daisy comes from hours spent with my two fuzzy fur balls. We share this planet with our pets—with *all* animals—and we owe them our best.

ACKNOWLEDGMENTS

The picture of a writer alone and struggling in an attic room might be a popular vision of how a book gets created, but it's inaccurate. Books are a team sport, and I owe many thanks to the following:

To Katie Bignell, who fell in love with Miss Daisy and thought others might, too.

To Ben Rosenthal, who adopted Miss Daisy and helped make her the lovable, thoughtful pooch she is now. Thank you to all at Katherine Tegen Books who helped groom Miss Daisy, including Janet Robbins Rosenberg, Amy Ryan, Kathryn Silsand, Joel Tippie, Mabel Hsu, and Katherine Tegen. Thank you for loving *A Dog Like Daisy*!

To Josh Adams, friend first and literary agent second, who believes in me every step of the journey.

Thank you to Josh, Tracey, Abby, and Jessie Adams.

To Ava Smith, the young neighbor who years ago said, "The guy who bred our Great Danes also breeds dogs who help veterans." That one conversation while our dogs were playing was the spark of this story. Thank you to Wade, Mary, Ava, Aubrianna, and Gavin Smith.

To Sylvester Criscone, my neighbor who said, "You know, I know someone who trains dogs to help veterans with PTSD." Thank you to Syl, Debbie, Mike, and Giana Criscone. Another thanks to Debbie for lots of laughter and baked goods!

(Yes, I have wonderful neighbors! Thanks, Kings' Chapel!)

To Katie Young, Syl's friend and the trainer with Southeastern Guide Dogs, who answered my many, many questions about dogs and training them to assist those with PTSD.

To Debbie Emory, writer friend and dog lover, who invited me to tag along and take notes while she and other trainers brought dogs to visit Monroe Harding Children's Home. Seeing how dogs light up the eyes of those who are struggling was invaluable.

To David Barberis, for his assistance in double-checking my Spanish grammar, and Jenny Rymer, my hometown friend who is immersed in and very knowledgeable about Mexican culture. Thank you for your help in making the Abeyta family and their celebrations come to life. My hope is that I've authentically captured the beauty and meaning of each one. Your help toward that end is much appreciated. Thank you to Jenny and her children: Ivan, Chloe, and Isaac.

To Robbie Bryan (Franklin, Tennessee), Kelly Flemings (Chattanooga, Tennessee), Jennifer Bailey (Bowling Green, Kentucky), and Barnes & Noble event planners nationwide: thank you for connecting books and readers!

To Stephanie Appell and all the awesome booksellers at Parnassus Books, and to independent bookstores and booksellers everywhere: thank you for building communities around the written word. And for shop dogs!

To school and public librarians like Lisa Rice, Ashley Fowlkes, Renee Hale, Lindsey Anderson, Julie Caudle, Sharla Bratton, Sheila Rollins, and many, many others: thank you for being mighty word warriors.

To the Society of Children's Book Writers and Illustrators, especially the Midsouth chapter. SCBWI paves the road ahead for writers and illustrators; this journey would be next to impossible (and FAR less fun) without you. Thank you!

To my critique group, who makes me laugh, cry, think, and write: you are like thick-cut, maple-spiced bacon. Thank you, Erica Rodgers, Courtney C. Stevens, and Rae Ann Parker. And Erica: thank you for both Micah and Miss Daisy; you are a name-picking genius.

To my family, the O'Donnells, the Grishams, the Goodmans, the Kites, and the Tubbs: thank you. You always offer prime rib–level support. With horserad-ish. And au jus. I love you.

To Byron, Chloe, and Jack: You are my every-thing.